Red Cape Publishing Presents...

The A-Z of Horror: A is for Aliens

DISCLAIMER: "This is a work of fiction. Names, characters, places and incidents are products of the author's imagination and are used fictitiously. Any resemblance to actual events, locales or persons, living or dead, is entirely coincidental."

Copyright © 2020 Red Cape Publishing

All rights reserved.

Cover Design by Red Cape Graphic Design

www.redcapepublishing.com/red-cape-graphic-design

Contents

Minor Constellations by Dona Fox	4
The Hazing by Theresa Jacobs	25
Alien Love by Nancy Kilpatrick	46
Communio by Daren Callow	63
Abducted by Astrid Addams	77
Buddy by Lesley Drane	104
Pike Street by Monster Smith	124
The Blue World by Jeremy Megargee	156
The Blagham Lake Ceremonies by Tim Jeffreys	172
Berserk by Mawr Gorshin	187
The Prairie Lures by Mark Anthony Smith	209
The Pioneer by P.J. Blakey-Novis	214
Even in Darkness, We See Them by Megan Neumann	236
Other Titles	263

Minor Constellations

Dona Fox

Ah, thank you, this pen writes much faster than that pencil, and I like the blue ink, it reminds me of Amy. But I should start at the beginning, and that would be when I was six when I first met Amy. I was small for a boy. But that didn't affect my brain, my whole family always said I was smart as a whip so I can guarantee every word of this confession is well-remembered, true, and correct.

This is my first time here in the city. I'm amazed you've covered everything with concrete and lit it up so bright you can't even see the stars. Seems you can't possibly know about magic anymore when you can't step out your door and pull a piece of tender stem out of a long sheath of grass to chew on while you ponder. Or just look up and let the twinkle of the stars and the soft glow of the moon hush your tumbling thoughts. Why, you can't even listen to the silence here, you don't have any left, it's buried beneath the roar of traffic and the jets cutting through your sky.

I pity you and Amy would too.

You see, Amy Fallenger was a star baby. That's what they would have called her in my neck of the woods in those days. They didn't realize how right they were. Your fancy doctors would have called her something else.

Those doctors tested her. I know because I was there when Mrs. Fallenger stopped their old Ford pickup on the gravel road by our farm to talk to my Mama. When Mama picked me up, all I could see was a bundle of blankets laying loose on the seat, squirming and whimpering, soft like.

"She's so quiet," Mama said, looking in the window of the truck.

"She's tired out," Mrs. Fallenger patted the pink bundle on the seat beside her, "they tested her blood, x-rayed her bones, and did a pile of other tests. She was real good. Hardly a sound out of her."

"Oh, you poor thing." Mama put her hand on Mrs. Fallenger's arm. "When will you hear something?"

"Well, they already determined she don't have the Downs or no defect in her heart or her little lungs. They said they can't find nothing wrong with my little Amy, except for the tinge of blue and the crusty white on her lips and eyelids, and on her teeny fingers." Mrs. Fallenger started to cry.

"Hey, now." Mama said, "that's good, right? They can't find nothin'."

"Yeah, yeah, that's good. Hank's gonna be upset anyway, he'll see it as a wasted day when I could'a been doing some work. He's gonna be mad. I better get home and have his dinner on the table." Mrs. Fallenger gave Mama a little wave and honked the horn as she drove off.

The next day Mrs. Fallenger came running through the fallow field that lay between our properties. She didn't care her shoes got muddy, and she didn't have a coat on. She was clasping Amy to her breast. Amy was wrapped in a thin dish towel despite the early April chill. The way Mrs. Fallenger was heaving sobs, I figured the child was dead.

But that wasn't the case.

Mama took the baby from Mrs. F and handed the bundle to me. "Lay her on my bed, put pillows all around her in case she rolls. Stay there, watch her." Amy was a fussy baby. I didn't like to hold her because she was so hot, and her heart beat fast inside her chest like a tiny baby bird.

I did as I was told, but I left Mama's

bedroom door open so as I could hear the conversation in the kitchen where Mama sat Mrs. Fallenger down at the table and poured coffee for them both.

"Sugar? Cream?"

"Yes, yes."

I could hear their spoons clinking against the sides of the china cups as the women stirred the sugar, cream, and heartache into their coffees. Clink clink clink clink. Like to drive me crazy. Pretty soon, Mrs. F quit sobbing.

"Now, tell me what's going on," Mama said.

"The doctor called." Clink clink clink.

"Yes?" Mama said. Clink clink clink.

"He told me Amy's condition is my fault. He said I poisoned Amy with our well water. Seems you can't mix a baby's formula with well water, or you might give them a thing called nitrate poisoning. Usually, this doesn't happen since most families with wells live more naturally, that's what he said, and too poor to buy infant formula, so the Mama's breastfeed their babies, he said that too. Shamed me. All of it shamed me."

"More coffee?" Mama said.

"Yes, please. I feel so guilty. Why didn't I breastfeed my baby? Why did I use well water in the formula? I poisoned my baby!"

"Shhh. Shhh." Mama made soothing sounds. "It's alright. Everything is going to be alright."

"What is Hank going to say? What will Hank do to me?" Mrs. F began to sob again.

"What do you mean, what will Hank do to you? If he does anything to you, you come to me." My Mama sounded real serious.

There was a pounding on the door, like to burst it in. We all jumped, and Amy started crying. It was Hank. Mr. Fallenger. He took his family home in the truck. He didn't honk neighborly as they drove off.

"Let me know," Mama called after them.

The doctor gave Amy some kind of shot. They said it saved her life, but it didn't take away the delicate hues. When I looked at Amy, I still saw tiny glowing blue and white fingers and azure lips, and I was afraid for her. It meant something, something that no one else could see.

The Fallengers asked me to babysit, so they could go into town. The first few times, especially the first time, I didn't want to, I was scared that Amy might die while I was in charge of her, but my parents made me do it.

I was careful with her, cautious as if she

were made of glass. She followed me with her eyes, and she laughed when I dropped the baby bottle. She had a bright, tinkling laugh, like a little bell. Something about her smile made me feel as if a clear spring had run through me and taken away all the bits of grime left by the day. I began to look forward to spending time with the child.

As Amy got older, she didn't talk, and they thought she couldn't get out of bed, her Mama was worried and her daddy was pissed. Amy smiled at me a lot, and she began to say words when we were alone, then she started fairly rattling off sentences at an unbelievable rate, but only when no one else was around.

Amy got out of her bed but only for me. At first, a few wobbly steps, like a newborn colt, just learning to walk, but I held onto her, and soon she was floating a foot off the ground, graceful as a butterfly. I swear it. But only for me.

With the medical bills and so many other stresses to contend with, the Fallengers fought a lot, and Mr. Fallenger was downright mean to Mrs. Fallenger.

I was about eleven when I stood up to him for the first time. I saw him slap Mrs. Fallenger. I was in the room, and I felt that made it my business. Plus, Amy was staring at me out of her bedroom from the bed that everyone thought she never left.

"You can't hit a woman," I said. First, Mr. Fallenger froze with his hand in the air, ready to strike again, then he pivoted toward me. He moved in slow motion as the air sucked out of the room, and I was about to pass out astounded at my own stupidity. I fully expected that unspent blow to land on me, but instead, he dropped his hand, threw back his head, and roared with laughter that was so loose and wild that it was more frightening than any calculated beating could have been.

When his laughter stopped, Mr. Fallenger wiped his face with his bare hand, then pulled out his giant handkerchief, blew his gnarled nose, and, finally, hitched up his belt. He cleared his throat as he carefully straightened one of the chairs at the kitchen table. Then he looked me up and down, from my floppy soled boots to my choppy back porch haircut. "Go home," he said, his voice way too calm.

I left, but when I looked back, I saw him throw that same chair he'd straightened so carefully all the way across the kitchen. The chair smashed into the far wall and fell in pieces to the floor along with the clock and half a dozen pictures of Amy at different ages, always smiling, showing her big shining teeth.

The next time I stood up to him, I was sixteen and full of myself. I was bigger, a tall beanpole, but I thought I was ready to take him on. I was just outside the door when I saw he had his wife pinned in a corner inside the house. He was slapping her with first one hand then the other in rotation. She couldn't get away, and her face was flaming red. Once again, Amy caught my eye from her dark bedroom.

Old Hank Fallenger must have decided he needed something from the barn because he left his wife trembling in the corner and headed out.

I cut around back and beat him there. He was surprised when I stepped out of the shadows.

"You can't hit a woman." My voice was soft, almost a whisper. I had my shovel in my hands.

"What did you say?" He swung toward me, a fist ready this time. "What did you say to me?"

I smiled because he had to look up to threaten me.

"I can't allow you to hit a woman," I said. Then I spit on the boards of the barn floor just because it was his property, and I prepared to raise my shovel.

A is for Aliens

Laughter didn't cloud his reason this time. I froze as pure anger, the same animal anger that seeped into the eyes of Ira our bull, before Mr. Fallenger charged me, blazed in my eyes. And just like Ira, Mr. Fallenger stomped his feet, and lowered his head, before he came at me. I swear I could see his horns and the flames shooting out from his nostrils.

Mr. Fallenger's assault knocked all the air out of my lungs. My feet flew out of my boots, my back hit the wall on the inside of the barn, then I slid down. My thin t-shirt offered no protection from the splinters that covered the inside of the unfinished planks.

Before I could catch a breath, Mr. Fallenger yanked me up by one of my wrists and drug me to that same nitrate-tainted well that poisoned his baby Amy. His dirty nails dug into my wrist while he used the other hand and his hip to push what Amy and I had calculated to be a five-hundred-pound cover comprised of iron and two by fours off the top of the well.

He tossed me in like I was a gunny sack full of spring kittens. As I fell, I heard the scraping of the cover, and darkness slowly filled the well like a dissipating moon.

Before pitch black set in, I spread my

arms and legs as wide as I could and managed to grab both the bucket and the corresponding rope used to pull the bucket up. The braids were slippery, and my hands were wet with fear. Still, I dug my fingers into the spaces between the twisted strands of the rope. I hiked my body up and squirreled around until I could gently lower my skinny butt into the bucket then I ratcheted as many fingers as possible through the other rope to equalize my weight. My whole body was shaking because I sincerely had no idea how I was gonna get out of Mr. Fallenger's creepy old well.

Gradually my body grew accustomed to the cold and damp. There were no monsters to be scared of, nothing jumping at me from the dark, so my mind settled on the fact of my upcoming slow death as there was nothing I could do about it. Maybe I should let go of the rope, toss aside the bucket, fall into the inky water, and drown. A quicker death. Just get it over with for it was surely comin'.

I must have dozed, when I opened my eyes, I startled and almost fell. I was so chilled my flesh felt like the silver bottom of the freezer.

The well was lit with a cold blue light. Amy was looking down, haloed by the full moon behind her. She laughed her beautiful laugh, and I felt better though I was still hanging inside the well.

"Let go of the other rope, hang on to the rope above the bucket, and I'll pull you up," she said.

"Oh, right, you'll pull me up." It was my turn to laugh.

"Hurry, Mr. Fallenger is coming back to the barn," she said, and I had no choice but to trust her.

Somehow, she pulled me up. I don't know if it was magic or something to do with the laws of fulcrums, I may have been playing hooky when they taught that stuff at school. When I was on my feet, she held out my shovel.

"Go home now, I'll see you soon," she said. But we both knew hell would have to freeze over a dozen times before Mr. Fallenger would let me back into his house again.

Then she kissed me on the cheek. And that did it.

I had to act before Mr. Fallenger started taking out his anger on Amy. I didn't know what had held him up this long. Because she was so small? Maybe he couldn't even see her. He never talked to her or even about her. He never looked in her direction. But she was getting older. Pretty soon, Mr. Fallenger would have to recognize her existence. And when he did, he was sure to realize the medical bills were her fault, and he would turn his fury on her.

"I will, I'll see you soon, Amy." I took my shovel and pretended I was going to cut across the field between our properties. But I didn't. I doubled back and hid right inside the barn door and waited for Mr. Fallenger.

This time he was shocked when I stepped out of the shadows. He'd put me in the well, under the five-hundred-pound cover.

"You can't hit a woman." Once again, my voice was soft, this time I made it sound like a ghostly whisper. I had my shovel in my hands behind my back. "There's a price to pay if you hit a woman."

"What? What did you say?" He backed away; he had no fist ready this time. "What did you say to me?" And then, almost a threat, "What price?"

I smiled because I still couldn't get over the irony, the humor in the fact that he had to look up to threaten me.

"You'll never hit a woman again. Never," I said slowly, letting the thought sink in.

When I could tell by the look in his eyes that he'd finally realized exactly what it would take to stop him from ever hitting his wife again, that's when I raised the shovel out from behind me and brought it down on his head. I think I might have clobbered him with the shovel more than once, but I'm not sure because a fit of red-hot anger roiled down and burnt my eyeballs.

Yep, I've heard people talking. The general consensus is that one night, Mr. F went out for a pack of cigarettes (or was it a loaf of bread?), and he never came home. You hear lots of stories like that around here where money is tight, so it isn't unusual for a man to take off, hop a train, duck his responsibilities, easy as pie.

I spent more time with Amy after that. She seemed sad, and our time was kind of bittersweet like she knew she was leaving soon. Like her purpose for coming was almost through.

Amy told me she didn't belong on Earth, that she died on her planet, and reconstituted here by mistake.

I cracked up laughing, and she held up her hand, icy blue palm toward my face, and gave me a hard look.

Suddenly her voice changed, deepened, grew husky, and I've got to say, it was frightening coming from that thin, blue-tinged body. "The one thing I will remember for the rest of this life is the feeling of dying. Yes, as converse as that sounds, dying is something you never forget. I imagine the feeling varies by person depending on the method of your demise, plus your level of readiness and acceptance."

"Come on, Amy, you're freaking me out," I said.

But she continued in that deep rough voice, "Last time I was ready for I had no other choice–I'd seen the future, and I knew that Ander's fingers would squeeze the life from my throat mere seconds before Shara's bullet would pierce his brain. Though I could not change events, I tried not to focus on her figure entering the apartment. I tried not to hear the almost silent scruff of her footsteps, the tiny click of her weapon, the whistle of the bullet cutting the silent air as my vision clicked off." Amy sighed and continued in her own voice, at least the voice I had come to know as Amy. "Anders had to die. He was a vicious man. Just like Hank Fallenger."

Amy stretched, her whole body was blue now, "It seems my sole purpose is to hop from planet to planet, effectuating the murder of those who must not be allowed to continue and ensuring the escape of

A is for Aliens

those I use as tools. At least this time I didn't have to die." She chuckled.

I stared at Amy until I realized my mouth was hanging open then I laughed, "You went from zero to hero real fast. It seems like yesterday you could barely talk, now you've become quite the storyteller. That was a good one."

"I'm not telling stories; I can prove it," she said. "Listen to me, and I might save your life. I felt Mr. Fallenger's body lying in the dirt on the other side of town. I felt the tiny insects, the grubs, the worms, nestling in, working, turning flesh and bones to liquid as the trains roared past nearby."

She had my complete attention as she continued, "I felt the gentle push of roots that wished to claim him, to encircle his remains and pull his nutrients into their cycle. I felt the rain seeping into the Earth, down to the hardpan beneath him, pooling there, lifting him. Stopping at the hardpan as you had to stop, surprised as you were to find hardpan on the hilltop, and your shovel not sharp enough, your arms not strong enough.

Though you had lifted and carried him with a strange supernatural strength born of desperation as the water now lifted him, up through the newly turned Earth. Lifted him and rolled him down the bank until he lodged against the train tracks.

And only the water streamed on. At least that's what I felt." She hunched her shoulders and held up her empty palms.

I said, "I'd better go look." I put on my dark raincoat and grabbed my shovel.

Sure enough, Mr. Fallenger's body had risen out of the shallow grave, rolled down the hill, and lodged against the train tracks.

Mr. Fallenger's entire body was swollen, especially his distended breasts and belly, which were now a deep blue-green. I had to smile, thinking Amy might enjoy the irony of his specific discoloration. He was mottled with dark blisters, and tiny holes pockmarked his skin.

After careful thought, I decided to pull him up the hill back to his grave. I crouched down, reached behind me, grabbed a wrist and ankle, and tugged. It must have been the pressure of the tug that did it.

It sounded like all hell broke loose behind me. I turned around and saw what looked to be his last few meals pouring from his mouth and streaming through his nostrils and possibly from every hole available on Mr. Fallenger's swollen body.

I covered my nose against the

unpleasant odors as I stood in awe. The blisters on Mr. Fallenger's body were popping from the strain I'd placed on his skin, and a foul, watery fluid poured out of them along with a stench unlike any I'd ever smelled before. But even that stench failed to equal the one that was coming.

Mr. Fallenger's huge belly rumbled as if he were still alive, or as if some wild animals were somehow trapped inside and fighting like crazy to get out. Then the backed-up meals shot like a geyser on a stream of gas that filled the air so horribly I liked to pass out on the spot despite my covered nose.

And worms crawled out of the tiny holes they'd bored in Mr. Fallenger's flesh. I prayed the rain would fall harder and drive the odor into the ground.

There was no way I was dragging Mr. Fallenger up the hill while fighting against the rain and the horrible odor of his decomposing body. But I couldn't leave him here. If he was found, they might, by coroner examination, trace his murder back to me. I was too young to die. And if they didn't trace his murder to me, they might, by logic, deduce Mrs. Fallenger as the culprit due to all the pain she'd suffered at his hands. No way could I let that happen.

A is for Aliens

As a matter of expediency, though the process involved many difficulties, I eventually rolled him onto the iron rail.

Anyway, I sat hidden, up on the hill, just on the verge of the trees, shivering in the rain, letting it wash the awful muck from my raincoat and the shovel I'd used as a lever, waiting for the train that would be my godsend.

Finally, right on time, the 2 AM express. Her whistle was joyous, and I thought I saw that old train wink at me in complicity when she ran him over, and he blew. Due to his previous state of deterioration, when she plowed through his body, it rendered him unidentifiable, or so I thought. Yet here I am.

Then I ran back to the house. I was laughing, that quiet laugh you do when you're practicing how you're gonna tell your best friend a funny story, a story that isn't complete until you share it with that one particular person. But Amy wasn't in her room. She wasn't waiting for me. Had she been out in the rain watching all the time? Was she just behind me? Should I run back and see?

Then I realized her room was more than empty. It smelled like an old unused attic room. Like no one had ever lived there, laughed in there, and told me stories of another planet.

In answer to my gentle questioning, Mrs. Fallenger didn't seem to remember ever having a baby. My Mama didn't remember Amy either. I was dumbfounded.

Well, that's my confession. I'm guaranteeing every word is true and correct, but I'm a minor without my Mama present, nor an attorney. And reading this may give you, by that I mean you all, cause to wonder if I have ever been totally in my right mind. And that would be another defense.

When I close my eyes, I still see tiny sparkling blue-white fingers and azure lips.

I'm not afraid for myself nor for Amy, as delicate as she was. I knew she was here for a reason, and she meant something to me, something that no one else would ever understand or believe. I look up in the sky and imagine she's one of the stars, and when I pinpoint which one, I will make a wish to join her.

***

Sheriff Mike Stone called his wife on the hands-free in his cruiser, "Hi, Honey. Can you hold supper up awhile? I'm on the way home, I just need to take a minute to look at the stars."

"Ha, you mean you're stopping for a cigarette?" his wife replied.

"Okay, you caught me." Mike smiled as he pulled to the side of the road. "I love you."

"Love you too," his wife said.

Mike leaned against the cruiser and smoked his cigarette. The kid's confession lay on the passenger seat.

Mike kicked a rock off the roadside into the field with his boot with every point he made in his mind: He'd checked, no one reported Hank Fallenger missing. There was no report of an incident on those railroad tracks. There were no birth records for Amy.

He lit another cigarette off the butt of the first one, perhaps he was working too hard. No one else had seen the kid walk into the station. When he reviewed the tapes of the interview, they were blank.

Mike left just long enough to get the kid a drink of water and when he came back to the locked interview room the kid was gone. The room was locked, dammit. He'd had to unlock it to get back in, he hadn't forgotten to secure it.

The kid was gone, but the confession lay on the table. He looked in the cruiser, he could see the white pages of the confession. He still had it.

He looked around for a long stem of grass to pull so he could chew on the juicy inside while he pondered, but there weren't any. Instead, Mike took a deep drag of his cigarette, leaned back, and looked up again. There were two stars, deep blue and twinkling, were they close to one another?

The Sheriff shook his head and chuckled as he climbed back into his cruiser. He rolled up the kid's confession and stuck it into the glove box. In the dim starlight, he failed to notice the pages were blank.

The Hazing

Theresa Jacobs

Marcus hooked his backpack over his shoulder, climbing from the car. "This is the easiest hazing I've ever heard of," he said.

"Yeah, you say that now, let's see how you feel at midnight!" Chris yelled from the backseat, followed by various other obnoxious taunts from the other frat roommates, Aaron and Bobby.

"What's so scary about this place, anyway? Looks like an old boarded-up house."

Chris leaned out the passenger window. "They say the family was found dead in their beds and all their insides were liquified."

"Yeah! And all the windows and doors were locked," Bobby shouted from the backseat.

Marcus scoffed, "Alrighty then, see you chumps in the morning." Turning from the car he headed up the cracked cement

A is for Aliens

path, his eyes absorbing the abandoned house. *It's just a house dummies*, he chuckled to himself. Ignoring their taunting calls from the street, he pulled back the plywood—the guys had ripped it from the doorframe under the cover of dawn—and squeezed through into the entranceway.

Pulling his iPhone from his jacket, he clicked on the flashlight, aiming it about the space. Dust coated everything and with each step a small plume rose into the air. Looking around the large open living room he was surprised that no one ever tried to break in before. The yellowed floral wallpaper showed its age in style.

The space was devoid of graffiti or the destruction of bored youths, or even the garbage of squatters.

"Boy, people must really be scared of this place," he said, peering around the frame into the 50s style kitchen, noting that even the appliances were intact. All he had to do was spend the night without leaving, while the three of his soon to be frat brothers would stay outside and watch, and if he did not set foot outside the house all night, he was initiated.

Marcus did not believe in ghosts; it

would be a simple night of watching Netflix on his tablet, and maybe sleeping a couple of hours. He checked through the empty rooms to reassure himself that he was indeed alone, and this wasn't some elaborate prank with other frat guys just waiting to spring out in the dark. Every nook, cranny, and closet were empty. The only place he was not about to check was the basement. Though not afraid, he wasn't dumb - basements were creepy.

However, he was in luck and the basement door had a latch (that was currently in the locked position) up near the top; he figured it would have kept any small children from falling down the stairs. Relieved that none of his buddies could sneak up on him in the wee hours, he moved to the middle bedroom, unrolled his sleeping bag, and propped himself up for a long, boring night.

***

It didn't take long for night to turn the room into inky blackness, and though it was early June, dampness settled throughout the barren home. Marcus had slid into the sleeping bag, already bored with his tablet. He found it odd how he could spend countless hours on the computer, and they would disappear like minutes, yet put into a place he didn't really want to be, the internet became uninteresting. With a heavy sigh he looked up into the dark rectangle of the open doorway. Because his eyes were adjusted to the light emitting from his screen, the hallway appeared as only a void.

Should I close the door? he wondered, waiting for his eyes to acclimate back to night. Shadows seemed to undulate against the wall outside the door. His breath held a second. "Relax," he whispered, "it's probably just light from cars passing by outside."

A loud squeal erupted from his lap. Marcus jumped; his tablet flipped upside-down. His heart paused a beat before it resumed beating too fast. Muffled laughter rang out next.

"Ah fuck," he cursed himself, realizing the noises were coming from the prank show he had been watching. He scooped up the iPad, checked the screen hadn't cracked, re-blinding himself to the dark space, and shut it off for the time being. The house plunged into silence. Marcus looked back out into the hall, staying motionless and listening. He knew the house was completely empty, but he hadn't thought to check and make sure all the windows were latched. He had no compunction about spending the night here, but he did not want the guys to sneak in and do anything stupid, like toss flash-bangs or something at him to scare him out either. Not hearing a peep, a floorboard creak, a whisper, or a giggle, he stood.

The bedroom he'd been told to spend the night in overlooked a small fenced-in side yard. It was unkempt and overgrown with tall grass and weeds. A half-moon did little to illuminate the space, so he stood with his back to the open door, staring into the yard for what felt an eternity. Not detecting any movement out there, he reached up to the top of the window frame and felt the metal latch tucked firmly in the lock position.

Room one done, he moved to the doorway where he halted again and looked out towards the other open doors. Soft light filtered across the dusty floor from the other two rooms, then darkness between, and the wider open space of the living room ahead. Walking softly, to keep an ear out for any movement within the house, he slipped into the master bedroom and paused. Through the window he could see his buddies leaning against the car, passing around a joint, holding beers, and laughing. He shook his head; they were going to get busted if they didn't clam up and get low soon. The entire neighbourhood wasn't a ghost-town and the suburbs didn't tolerate college kids goofing off in the dead of night.

Not wanting them to spot him at the window, he stayed close the wall and followed it around until he was against the same wall. Standing on his toes, he peeked over at the top of the window, seeing the latch here too was locked. Thinking about it now, it did make sense that all the windows were safely locked otherwise kids, or meth-heads, surely would have trashed the place already. But having lots of time to kill, he figured he'd continue.

The last bedroom overlooked the backyard. It too was a mess of tall grass and weeds. Only it housed a metal shed which stood open and seemed empty. He couldn't be sure from his vantage point, but all the contents of the house were gone, so it made sense. It had nothing to do with his current situation; he just had nothing better to think about, other than what the real story was. He didn't believe his roommates for one second. "I wonder what really happened?" Marcus said, feeling melancholy all of a sudden.

Shaking it off, he headed back to the kitchen. The latch was still set on the basement door. He grasped the small knob on the slide-bolt, lifted it to the up position and it squealed in protest causing goosebumps to raise the hair on his arms.

He groaned at the sound and set the latch back down, deciding it too rusted to attempt.

The backdoor was locked up tight with the security chain and deadbolt both in place. With nothing left to check, (he knew he'd hear if the guys fiddled with the plywood across the front door), he returned to his room for the night. Only this time, he closed the door behind himself and resettled into the sleeping bag.

***

A is for Aliens

Marcus's conscious rose with the need to pee. He was warm, but not comfortable and when he moved to readjust his pillow, his elbow clunked against the hard floor and the challenge came flooding back to the forefront. Blinking and trying to remove the gummy feeling from his mouth at the same time, he saw it was morning twilight. Not wanting to check the time on his phone just yet, as the bright screen would once again blind him, he climbed out the bag stretching his aching joints.

Thinking about how much he was going to rub it in to the guys that they just wasted an entire night of their lives, he stumbled out towards the bathroom. Even though the toilet wouldn't work, he didn't care, a drain was a drain, and he'd already pissed into the tub twice that night, once more wouldn't hurt. He propped his shoulder against the wall and let his stream flow into the tub, yawning. The hair over his ear moved. He shuddered with the sensation of a tickle, and the image of a spider crawling across his face gave him deep shivers. Swiping at his face, his fingers encountered what felt like a wet macaroni noodle stuck in his hair. He screamed and jumped back, shaking his

A is for Aliens

head. The thing oozed, too fast for him to grasp, across his brow and down his nose.

"*What the fuck!*" he screeched, slapping himself in the face. Spinning in a wild dance of fear and disgust, he caught a glimpse in the dull bathroom mirror as a blue tubular-shaped thing swooped up his nostril. He fell to knees, plugged one side of his nose and blew. The thing felt fat, blocking his airway. He gagged and tried hocking it out while shaking his head as though that would help dislodge it. His eyes rolled back, and he passed out.

The blue thing made itself at home.

***

Groaning, Marcus opened his eyes to a narrow ivory cupboard. "Huh?" he said, blinking perplexed at the view. He lifted his head and saw the sink and tub ahead. "Ow, what?" He sat up, noticed his flaccid penis hanging out of his pants and recalled peeing in the tub. Standing, he tucked himself away and looked around. The last memory he had was of the tub and then nothing. *Weird*, he thought, and saw bright sun streaming down the hallway. He mumbled 'fuck it' and went to gather his belongings.

Aaron nudged his slumbering buddy beside him in the front of the car. "Hey, here he comes."

"Huh?" Bobby groaned, shaking himself awake.

"Whoow!" Chris hooted. "Marcus!"

"Get in here bro." Aaron waved Marcus to the car, leaning between the front seats to congratulate the fraternity member as he climbed into the backseat.

"You did it, man! Was it..." he halted as Marcus bent his head into the car. A thin membrane, much like a lizard's eyelid, flashed closed vertically below Marcus's normal eyelid. Aaron pulled back from the space between the front seats and faced forward. Perplexed, he shook it off as too many beers.

Marcus finished Aaron's sentence, "Boring? Long? Uncomfortable? All of the above!" He laughed. "Easiest bet ever. Home James!"

"So, what? Nothing, bro?" Chris asked, slouched in the back seat looking a little worse for wear.

"What? In there?" Marcus replied watching the house ease away as the car turned a corner. "Nothing whatsoever."

"Bummer," Chris replied and burped.

***

"Pippin!" Aaron scooped up the house mascot, a wild-haired terrier, planting kisses all over its furry face.

"Quit mauling the dog." Bobby punched Aaron in the shoulder. "I swear you'd make him your girlfriend if it was a bitch."

Aaron continued to cuddle the little beast who was loving every moment of it. "I just miss my own dog back home," he defended, "nothing wrong with that. Hey, watch it!" He cocked his head as Chris pushed through the guys and ran down the hall. They all burst out laughing when vomiting sounds reached their ears.

Marcus yawned. He thought he'd slept fairly well in the house, but his entire body ached, and he felt like a walking zombie. "On that note, I'm off to get some sleep," he said, taking the stairs two at a time.

"Good idea. Right Pips?" Aaron headed off with the dog.

"Pussies!" Bobby called, taking to the couch and flipping on the television.

"Not you too?" he moaned as Chris

came from the bathroom looking grey

"Oh yeah, see you in a few." Was all Chris managed as he slouched past the couch towards the stairs.

***

Comfortable in his bed, Marcus dreamed strange things. His mind awakened to the comfort and unity of an infinite consciousness. Singularity slipped away as he writhed in a seething mass of others like him. Unearthly sounds whispered from a million voices and he understood their calling. They were trying to bring him home, and he longed to go. He needed them and they needed him. "Home," he mumbled, turning in his bed, his eyes opening to the small boxy room that most certainly was not home.

His thoughts came from somewhere that were not his own. Marcus knew this but couldn't stop it. Disembodied, he watched his feet slip out of bed and touch the floor, out of his control. Pain reached every nerve ending, yet he was powerless to react. His head spun towards the closed door that did little to block out the sounds of snoring. *Food,* his invader said, and

Marcus wanted to scream, *No!*

Instead, he watched the door open.

Entering Chris's bedroom, the Marcus-thing leaned over the sleeping form. The scent of stale beer and vomit invaded his flaring nostrils. Yanking the covers back, he moved in beside the hot body. His skin rippled like the surface of a lake in a gentle breeze—in anticipation of what was to come.

The sleeper moaned at the intrusion; the Marcus-thing rolled directly on top of the young man. His arms and legs wrapped around the pliable human and he began to squeeze.

Chris's eyes flew open. At first, they registered confusion, flashing to terror as he saw Marcus's face hovering inches above his own. A scream formed as he looked into eyes that were not Marcus's baby blues, but blood red, with vertical yellow pupils. All he managed was a high pitched, "eeeeee", as the arms around him squeezed. His ribs snapped, pop, pop, pop. One after another. His eyes bulged with agony as both his arms cracked, then his hips. He keened breathless, helpless.

A tube wriggled out of Marcus-thing's mouth, pressing against the other man's lips. They parted unwillingly, allowing the tube into his throat. It suckled greedily.

Marcus's mind snapped as whatever was living inside of him ate his friend's insides and blessed blackness took over.

When the body of food stopped convulsing, the Marcus-thing released it and slithered to the floor.

From the hallway, Pippin barked, scratching at Aaron's door.

"Gotta go pee Pips?" Aaron said, opening his door to let the dog out and stepping into the hall, stopping in his tracks. "What the fu...?" Marcus was lying on the floor and pulling himself along somehow without using his hands or legs. Before Aaron could comprehend what was happening, Marcus pressed off one knee and leapt onto the stuttering frat brother.

Aaron moved left to sidestep Marcus but was caught mid-stride as the weight of the other man hit him, and they both tumbled sidelong down the stairs. Aaron screamed as they thudded, bumped, and rolled together in a heap.

"What's going on?" Bobby yelled, coming from the living room to see the ruckus. "Hey! Are you guys..." his heart skipped a beat when Marcus looked up from atop

Aaron. A fat blue tube flopped out of his mouth against Aaron's cheek, and his eyes looked all wrong. "Bloody hell!" he said, then spun, running to the kitchen.

Aaron moaned, letting out a huff. He felt pressure around his ribs. His eyes flew open now, recalling Marcus on him, squeezing him ... and those eyes!

Pippin ran up to the thing that was hurting his best friend and barked with the fury only small dogs possessed. Marcus's hand flashed out grabbing the mutt.

Aaron screamed, "*No! Leave the dog alone, you bastard!*"

The tube projected out of Marcus-things' mouth and directly into the yipping maw of the dog. His hand released, and Pippin turned tail, booking it out of the room. Instantly Marcus went limp, falling sidelong. His head bounced off the floor and Aaron pushed out from under his legs.

Bobby had returned from the kitchen with a gun and stood dumbfounded, pointing at the pair on the floor.

"Too late Bobbo," Aaron wheezed, "now we gotta find Pippin."

"Is he..."

A is for Aliens

Aaron leaned towards Marcus, giving him a quick poke in the side. "I think so, yeah."

"Did you see that? What was it?"

"I don't know, do I look like fucking Kreskin?"

Bobby waved the gun towards the hallway. "Well it killed Marcus and now it's in Pippin, why don't we just leave and let the cops deal with it?"

"Pippin?" Aaron called. "Here Pips." He turned to Bobby. "Quit being such a pussy. What are you gonna tell the cops? We forced our friend to stay the night in a haunted house, but instead he returned with a killer parasite?"

"Nuh, that ain't no parasite man, it's an alien! Haven't you ever seen *The Thing*? Or *Aliens*? It came shooting outta him like a beast," Bobby whined.

"All the more reason not to let it escape. Let's get it."

Aaron grabbed a baseball bat from the hall closet and together they stood staring into the living room. The furnishings were sparse. They owned a ratty couch from the 80s era, a 60-inch flat screen TV that sat on a black glass console, a torn leather and duct-taped recliner, and a full-sized pool table. The small dog was nowhere to be seen.

"Pip?" Aaron said again, quieter than before.

"Where is it?" Bobby whispered.

"Go look behind the curtains," Aaron suggested.

Bobby scoffed, "No fucking way, you go."

A whimper came off to their right, and both heads swivelled. Aaron nodded.

"It's over by the tree." No one else would call it a tree. It may have been a tree at one time, or rather perhaps eventually grown into a tree, only now it was a large dead stick in a pot of petrified soil because the frat boys never watered it; many even used it as a urinal at parties. The whimper came again, and its small black nose peeked out from behind the pot.

"Aw, he's hurting," Aaron moaned.

Bobby shoved him into the room. "Okay, you love it, go put an end to its misery then."

Aaron elbowed back, though continued into the room, walking slow, one foot sliding along, followed by the other. He hunched forward, closer to the ground. "Come here Pips, I'll make you feel better pup-pup." He glanced at the bat in hand and had the flash of whacking the dog over the head. Its small trusting brown eyes would look at him with horror and wonder why one who loved him so would want to hurt him. Aaron straightened, lowering the bat. "I can't do it Bo…"

The dog leapt from its hiding place. Aaron saw a flash of white as it shot past his head. Bobby screamed and shot the gun wildly into the air.

"*Son-of-a-bitch*!" Aaron cried out, ducking. A hot streaking pain caught his arm, and he grabbed at the hot spot, while simultaneously spinning and ducking.

Bobby got a few shots off before the gun flew from his grip as he braced against the speeding dog. He tripped back, hit the edge of the doorway and fell directly onto his back. The yipping dog was clutched in both hands and wriggling to beat the band. "*Get the gun! Hurry! Kill it!*" he hollered, keeping his mouth turned away from the dog's.

"You shot me, you bastard," Aaron cried as he regained his footing and dove after the spinning weapon.

"J-u-st *help!*"

The small dog kicked air. The eyes

transformed as Marcus's had, to red slits. Its mouth opened, only not to bark, the blue tube jabbed forth stabbing at Bobby's face, trying to gain access inside. "Ughh," he grunted.

"Hold still," Aaron called. His voice was followed by a pop and wood chips ricocheting into Bobby's face.

Bobby screeched at bullets whizzing by his head and he flung the dog at the wall. It hit with a loud thud, yelped, and lay still. The blue tube flopped from the dog's mouth and shimmied up the wall.

"*Get it! There*," he said, pointing. The gun popped, bits of drywall, dust, and wood flew into his face. Holding a hand up, he shrieked again, ducking away from the exploding wall. The blue thing took advantage of his open mouth and dove. Bobby's eyes widened, he clutched at his throat, spinning towards Aaron.

"Sorry bud," Aaron said, taking one more shot.

Bobby didn't have time to react. A hole opened above one eye and he fell back into the wall, still holding his throat.

"Shit," Aaron huffed. His hands were shaking wildly, and he struggled to keep the gun tight. The room seemed to ring from the shots, and he thought he heard sirens in the distance, but wasn't sure. He kicked Bobby's foot. "Bobbo?" he said, watching for any movement from his mouth. Nothing happened. He moved closer. Bending to peer into the black hole, he wanted to see if the blue tube was there, or if it too died with the bullet. Using the gun's muzzle, he pulled down Bobby's bottom lip. Something shifted across the floor behind him. Aaron screamed, jumped back away from the body, and saw Pippin trying to stand. Sirens grew louder as they entered the neighbourhood. He was both relieved and terrified; after all, he'd just shot one of his roommates.

"Pips, come here baby," he cooed, reaching out for the dog. The dog whined, unable to stand. Aaron slid closer, letting his fingers caress the dog's back. The big sad brown eyes looked up at him and he knew it was safe now. "It's okay, Pips, help's coming. We'll be alright."

The sirens were right outside, doors slammed, and voices rang out.

"Come on, Pips, let's get help." Aaron placed his hand under the dog's belly. It retched, causing Aaron to let go with a scream.

The door burst open as thousands of miniscule blue worms vomited from the dog's mouth.

Alien Love

Nancy Kilpatrick

My lover is an alien. Not a person from another culture, but a being from another planet.

Many women feel that way about men, of course, and vice versa; it's a statement of how disparate the genders often seem to one another. But that's not what I'm talking about. I'm talking about a *real* alien. A being unlike any other that walks this planet.

I'm not a patient in a mental hospital, writing this on scraps of toilet paper, and I'm not some SoHo performance artist who wants to shock and enlighten. I'm just a woman, an ordinary human being. And because of destiny, I managed to hook up with Thomas, or at least that's the name I call him, since the sounds he makes are enough like that name that I find it comfortingly familiar.

From the start I'll admit that I've always had a fascination with extraterrestrial life.

A is for Aliens

That may taint some of what I'm about to say. Even though the majority of North Americans, if not citizens of this planet, believe that intelligent life exists in space, admitting to that seems tantamount to implying eccentricity at best and lunacy at worst. I will also acknowledge that I went through a period of time—about a year actually—when my marriage was breaking down where I'd drive around Philadelphia at night in my little silver Toyota searching the skies. Of course, as Fox Mulder would have been the first to tell us, a city is the last place where a spaceship would land. The fact that I, like most people, know that, didn't stop me from looking. But then I was close to a breakdown. Whenever I traveled on business or for pleasure, I'd rent a car and drive around—in Atlanta, in Phoenix, in Stanford, Connecticut. I did not see any ships or any aliens. I was not a passenger on one of the commercial aircraft where the pilots saw alien vessels trailing their Boeings. I did not visit that town in the Yukon where the entire population saw lights that were not the aurora borealis streak across the sky for several nights in a row. I have never been aboard an alien craft, either

A is for Aliens

voluntarily or as a kidnap victim, and have not be the subject of alien medical probes. At least not that I remember.

That year of searching the skies was an anomaly in my life. And when the divorce was finalized and I began to heal emotionally, I read Carl Jung and something he said, about spaceships and extraterrestrial life being symbolic of a search for the divine and a latent desire for wholeness, well, that made sense to me.

Besides Jung, I read a lot of science fiction. From the novels and short stories there seems to be several theories as to why these beings come to Earth. Foremost is to make contact. Another reason is to keep tabs on us, the techno-idiots of the universe. To invade our planet and take it and its citizens for their own is a third, and to intermingle and create a new species is last but not least. But I've discovered another reason they come here; at least with Thomas that seems to be so.

We met in Toronto. I was there on business, staying at one of the chain hotels on Lake Ontario where the computer conference was being held. It was summer, a pleasant evening, and I decided to take a walk along the harbor of this notoriously safe city.

The sun had just set, but the sky was still light. Cars sped by on the above-ground roadway behind me, far enough in the distance to not be annoying. As I gazed out over the lake, boats with white sails dotted the water, and I watched the ferry boats carrying people back and forth between the mainland and a five-mile strip of terra firma called Toronto Island. I walked slowly along the flag-stoned harbor path breathing deeply the fresh air and stopped to rest against the ropes that acted as a barrier between land and water.

We've all had that feeling, of someone staring at our back. In the twilight, I sensed him and turned to my right. Coming along the path was a man with white hair and wearing a white suit. He was not old, but in his late thirties, my age, or so it seemed to me then, although then, as now, I cannot clearly recall his face; he possesses a timeless quality. His body emitted some type of invisible energy that drew my attention. I know that sounds very New Agey, but believe me, other than that year of living dangerously close to the border of breaking apart, I normally have my feet firmly planted on the ground.

When he reached me, he just stopped and turned, so that he, too, stood facing the water. It was as though we were old friends who didn't need words to communicate with one another. We simply stood there, inches apart, shoulders almost the same height.

Now, I do not normally talk with strangers, except in a crowded place, like a bank, or a restaurant lineup, or at a business conference, and then it's cursory and polite, the conversation pointed. I'm not paranoid, simply cautious. Being in a strange city usually inspires extra caution. And since there were no other people along the waterfront, at any other time I would have walked away.

Why did I stay there? I've thought about that a lot. There's the obvious—I was lonely. But loneliness has never been enough reason to cause my good sense to abandon me before, other than my search for spaceships, and I think I've explained that. With all the pondering I've done, though, I still can't honestly say what kept me there, other than that I felt something happening that I liked. It was as if the level of iron in my body had been seriously depleted and I hadn't been aware of it. Then, suddenly, my receptors were open and reaching out towards this being to be replenished. I know that sounds vampiric of me, and I suppose that our relationship is like that in a way. But there's more to this relationship. Much more.

But that first evening, we stood at the water's edge until the sky darkened and the new moon rose. I was keenly aware of him, the power of the energy that pulsated from him. That intensity left me afraid to actually look at him. But when I did turn, he turned also, mirroring me, as if he were a mime. I stared into pale almond eyes that seemed to darken then lighten as I watched them. They enlarged and emitted a warmth that cocooned me from head to toe. Had he touched me physically the sensations could not have been stronger. I found myself gasping, overwhelmed by a kind of passion I had not envisioned existed. It was like orgasming on the sidewalk, and I was both afraid and excited.

Suddenly, he turned. Whatever energy connected us, connected us still. As he walked away, I was pulled along, behind him, by invisible bonds.

We walked and walked, as far as the harbor path would take us, then through a park, then to a marina. At the far end he boarded what I can only describe as a black metallic vessel that blended with the night, so well, it seemed to be invisible. I trailed behind him up the midnight gang plank, my heels clacking against the metal, still engulfed by silky yet invisible threads of passion kneading me. Once down below deck, he shut the door and we were plunged into complete darkness.

It was at this point that I became aware of being very afraid. I've never felt comfortable in the dark, and there I was, in a peculiar, isolated place, with a stranger, in a strange city. I tried to speak but found I couldn't form words. I imagine this is what aphasia feels like: you know the concept you are trying to get across but can't quite remember how to say the words. Although I was not physically bound, I might as well have been, because I was unable to move.

My eyes became accustomed to the metallic blackness. I couldn't actually see anything identifiable, but I had vague impressions, one of which was this man—

for a few moments more I still thought of him as just a man—standing there, facing me, silently. I realized my heart was beating hard, and my lungs were filling and expanding rapidly. Chilly sweat coated my body, and my limbs trembled.

I wanted to ask him what he was doing to me that left me immobile. I wanted to know why he had brought me here and what he had planned. I wanted to know who, no *what*—because by then I began to realize that he was not quite human. I wanted to ask him why he had no scent. Of all the other questions, that was the one that startled me most when I became aware of it. I simply could not smell him. Stainless steel has a smell. Even plastic has an odor. And certainly anything organic. But he did not. And although my own sense of smell has never been outstanding, it isn't bad and I recognized that scent was the one sense missing.

Finally, when I thought my heart might not be able to take the tension any longer, a sudden wave of calm rolled over me. I realized he was flowing closer—that I *could* sense.

Oddly enough, the closer he got—as he had at the harbor—the more my anxiety turned to pleasure, and the pleasure to passion. When he reached me physically, I gasped.

He lit up—that's the only way I can put it—phosphor in a metallic night sky. The light took the shape of his body, but more than his body, as if what the psychics call an 'aura' was visible and his solid molecules actually mingled with the air molecules and I could see no clear division between them. There were colors I recognized, but many I did not, as though he used a different spectrum and my eyes could finally see what they normally were unable to distinguish. Colors that had the intensity of red and yet were more like combinations of blackened silver and yellow and peach, although that does nothing to describe them or do them justice. I found the visuals fascinating. So much so that I did not at first realize that his body was enfolding mine. The colors that he vibrated encased me and then I felt them enter every pore in my flesh. But they entered me as a scent, like thousands of tiny vapors working their way into every pore. The scent was new to me, more pungent than sweet or tart, greater than anything I had encountered before. It was a penetration I could not have envisioned and one that kept me on the edge of something akin to climaxing in a delicious, delirious state of almost being sated. A state where time and space became meaningless and all that mattered was this essence that filled my body through my pores as, by way of a poor analogy, the smell of roses would have filled my nasal cavities and lifted my spirits. And through it all I heard him. And yes, it is likely that in my fragile humanity I reached out and used the sounds to form a name, to find something familiar...

In the morning—and I must skip to daybreak because I cannot honestly remember details—I found myself lying on the path at the harbor where I'd first seen him. There was no sign of him. No sign that he had even been there. And, of course, my sanity returned. With it, anxiety surged. It wasn't long before I was at a police station, filing a complaint with them, trying to describe a man I could not remember visually with a crime that seemed like rape but which I could not articulate.

A is for Aliens

I scanned hundreds of photos. The dark metallic ship was gone, of course. The police dusted the harbor ropes for fingerprints and found only mine. And the worst part of it all was that a physical examination revealed no signs of intercourse. I couldn't bring myself to tell them that the entry had been through my pores as well as every orifice of my body, but I did ask for a skin analysis. Nothing unusual showed up. And by the time the DNA results of blood and vaginal secretions finally came through, I was back home. Only my own DNA was present.

That encounter occurred a year ago. I went through much trauma and soul-searching. I even saw a psychiatrist for a few sessions—until the next new moon.

Every month, at the first sliver of a moon, Thomas shows up, no matter where I am. I could be home alone in my living room. At a movie with friends. Working overtime. Traveling again. Each time it is the same. I am drawn to him, as if my body needs to recharge. He takes me someplace where we can be alone. And I go willingly. And then he is recharging as well, with what he gets from me, through my pores, whatever that is. I still don't know.

I have been afraid. Utterly terrified to be precise. Never with him, but between the times when I see him. And what terrifies me most is how much I long for him.

It took me three months to realize it was the moon that determined when he would appear, which leads me to feel that the moon plays on him as it plays on our tides. Perhaps his home is a moon, black and metallic. It took time to realize the symbolism of that beginning the new moon represents. It took time for me to realize exactly how I have changed.

Needless to say, I am different. Whereas once I was outgoing, now I live only for those hours when I am with Thomas. I am obsessed, yet to my family, friends and colleagues I am the same woman I have always been. I go about my business and interact in familiar patterns. But my life is like an orange with the juice extracted from it. When we are together Thomas gives to me, but he also takes from me and in his wake leaves behind an ever-hollowing shell. Oddly enough, I do not hold this against him. Somehow, it makes me love him more.

Physically, I am constantly dehydrated. That, of course, leaves me exhausted, but then, as the new psychiatrist says, I'm depressed, and the anti-depressants do not help. I have many of the symptoms of HIV and yet the tests are negative, and no virus can be isolated. The doctors are stymied by that, and more so by what they have labeled a noxious odor my body emits. The colors with their wondrous fragrance that Thomas leaves inside me seem to transform into something not so pleasant to others. To hear people talk, you would think I was rotting inside, and one day I will wake up and be nothing but decay. But the decay smells sweet to my nostrils, because it reminds me of him.

And Thomas? Each time I see him I know he is stronger. His colors smell brighter, more vivid, and their range has expanded the spectrum of hues. He lives while I die. It seems unfair, and yet what he gives me is all that has meaning in my life. All that keeps me going. All that matters. And I would gladly give him every drop of my existence for one more breath of that alien scent.

It amazes me now that I spent an entire year searching the heavens for aliens when one was walking this planet. Is that why he found me, because I searched for him? What he shows me I realize is his home planet, which must be so far away, perhaps in another galaxy, or even another time or dimension. I do not know exactly why he has left there and come here, but I feel he is the only one of his kind and that he has found a way to survive. I feel, too, his loneliness. Except for me he has no contact, although I could be wrong. It's possible that every night he absorbs the essence of another who acts like a battery providing him energy until the battery itself dies and is either recharged, or a replacement is found. But I don't think so. I think that it is *my* essence he wants and needs, and my greatest worry is what he will do when I'm gone. Because I know in my heart that he does not understand death. On his planet, wherever he comes from, life continues in black-star darkness, an ever-changing form. It is simply a matter of revitalizing. He cannot know that we poor mortals who strive for wholeness do so in order that we might blend with the whole, with the divine, with what is larger than us and we hope will absorb us when our frail bodies can no longer contain who we are.

What I have come to understand is that as he takes me in, I take him in, and it's possible that internally he is changing as I am. Why do I think that? Because I can now smell him. And he smells sweet. Very, very sweet. The sweet essence of all life itself, the life of this planet Earth. It makes sense to me; that's why he has come here. To take me in.

Communio
Daren Callow

To start with they only came at night.

At least I assumed they did, as that's when I first saw them, standing motionless beyond our perimeter fence. There were two of them, all in black, head to toe, assuming they were creatures that had toes of course. The apparitions seemed to be nearly twice my size in every direction, although almost impossible to make out in the ink-black prairie gloom. For myself, I was exhausted and struggling from a long day tending the animals, and at first, I thought perhaps my tired mind was playing tricks on me. I was content to convince myself as such and I fell into an uneasy sleep. However, when I returned to the window, with much trepidation I should tell you, the following morn, half hoping to see a tree or other flotsam brought in on the wind that might account for the apparitions, there was nothing but flat earth and dust.

I made my way out, clutching a

homemade sports bat I'd always kept under the bed, but found no discernible trace of visitors. There were scuff marks on the ground, but they could easily have been from my herd, who roamed every which way you like looking for a little scrub to eat. Nevertheless, I spent the day fretting and made doubly sure all my animals were safely in the pen well before the sun sunk below the horizon that evening. But the figures did not return that night nor, to my growing relief, the next two nights neither. However, just as I was beginning to relax back into my routine, they returned on the third night, in pretty much the same spot.

Since I had been half-expecting them on this second visitation, despite my shaking, I took a little time to study them, my heart pumping hard whilst I peered through the gloom. As previously surmised, the two silhouettes were odd and intimidating, without doing anything really threatening. Their black coveralls, at least I assumed they were such, obscured every inch of them, starting with a dome-like hat that covered their features, and ending in boots the same width as their lower coverings. So, it was hard to discern where leg ended,

A is for Aliens

and foot began. Again, they simply stood and observed me, presuming they were looking my way, it was hard to tell, as I observed them. Somehow, I managed to convince myself that from their positioning - on a little rise - that the spot had been chosen to allow them to see into the compound. Their height was hard to judge given the darkness and the distance from the ranch, but I continued to believe that they were probably twice my height at least.

Now I am willowy even for a rancher, who are usually the wiriest of the wiry. But I'd never before felt scared in my own acre as I did now. Sure, we have predators that pay us the odd visit, but our stone compound walls, and electric fence keeps them a bay. The need for a weapon had never occurred to me before. The night-time visits changed all that though, and I resolved to ride into town at the first reasonable opportunity and acquire one.

By noting their infrequent appearances in a small journal, it soon became clear that they definitely did not approach on nights when the moon shone brightly. This being known, I resolved to depart the following day for the town in the knowledge that it was a fair night with a full moon. Even if I returned late, I should be unmolested, at least that is what I hoped.

So, the next day I rode the long ride into the nearest town. Now it must be said, that my life and beliefs having been stood on their head by my nightly hauntings, so it was almost as disturbing to me to find that the town was completely unaffected, and business carried on relentlessly without any discernible change. I went directly to the gunsmith and acquired myself an old, but perfectly serviceable, projectile weapon and a couple of boxes of ammunition. It was all I could afford, but I presumed it to be effective enough to ward off the devils of the night. If they were indeed wearing magical suits to keep them alive on our world, then a few holes would certainly get them thinking. Or so I hoped.

The gunsmith, having seen it all before, asked no questions and so I had no opportunity to explain my predicament. The same could not be said of the saloon bar. Here, after more than a few glasses of moonshine with my fellow ranchers, the banter was free-flowing, and it was no small relief to unload my freaky tale.

A is for Aliens

Whilst most dismissed my monologue as whimsey or too far-fetched to be credible, a wanderer from out of town ventured that he had indeed heard talk of sombre golems that came in the dead of night. I engaged him further, but found the conversation soon taking a direction I did not relish as much.

It seemed in his understanding the monsters tended to take observations for a few nights before returning mob-handed to take away the farmer, or other unfortunate, for unspeakable examinations with probes and other intrusions of an intimate nature. Before returning them to their beds their minds wiped of all but a few fractured details, to be derided by all who came to hear the telling.

This seemed to spark recollections in others and soon the conversation turned to strange lights in the night sky, flying disk-shaped machines and more tales of abduction and examination. In due course someone ventured that the giants were not from this world at all, but actually aliens from somewhere else in firmament. Others dismissed these suggestions, venturing instead that it was probably the government up to no good, or a previously undiscovered tribe of indigenous giants, or simply the ravings of notorious drunkards.

However, the tales of freaks and off-worlders resonated more deeply with what I'd observed and by now I was so utterly terrified that I found myself imbibing more hooch than I cared to recall. I felt too afraid to return home that night, despite the full moon, and had to pay for a room at a local hostelry that was more than I could really afford. There I spent a fitful night concerned as much for my animals, half a day's ride distant, as my own personal safety when I returned to my homestead.

The following day I made the long journey back, nursing a sore head, but my fears quenched by a bright sun that seemed to dispel, for a few hours, any notion of ghostly alien visitations. My newly acquired firearm was also a small comfort. Despite that, I found myself dreading the creeping return of night. True to form, however, and perhaps to make me seem as ridiculous as possible, I was not haunted that evening.

In fact, it was nearly two weeks before I saw them again, and in this time, something had clearly changed. If I didn't know better, I would have to assume that they were aware that I had a weapon now. Instead of their simple bipedal shape they now were equipped with what seemed to be round shields of some description and bent sticks that could easily have been weapons of some alien manufacture. There were also more of them. Two at the usual spot and two more, shields held high standing near to the electric wire fence. Were they looking for a way in? My heart clamoured hard against my ribs and I fumbled with my rifle, only now wishing I'd spent more time learning to shoot when I had been younger.

Nevertheless, I got the gun loaded and pushed open the window to train it on the nearest of the monsters. Now it seemed that they were clearly aware of me, and for the very first time I saw them move! There were noises too as I struggled to keep a bead on them in the pitch black. The nearest two figures retreated rapidly, with a speed in excess of what I would have thought them capable. One held the shield aloft whilst the other brushed furiously at the ground with some sort of broom, clearly intent on covering their tracks. No golems these, they clearly had a plan and were working together to achieve it. All the same, I was glad to see that they seemed, perhaps, to be as afeard of me as I was of them. Still I was only one and, surely, they would return again in even greater numbers.

That night I slept with my weapon in my arms in the way that I had heard the first settlers had often done. It gave me little comfort.

The next morning all seemed quiet and again I found myself questioning my sanity. Had I simply dreamt it all, spurred on by the banter of strangers and lingering alcohol? It was all too odd, too utterly strange that I really did wonder if I was under some sort of spell, or simply losing my mind. Events later that day brought me back to earth with a jolt. Whilst doing my final rounds of the day I came across the carcass of one of my cattle, dead and clearly violated in a sickening and unnatural way, or at least that's what my fevered mind told me. It was split open from neck to udder, organs laid out here and there in what seemed to be some kind of pattern. No carnivore had done this; surely this was a dissection, a biological examination, no more, no less. A superior being casually rendering down things that they wished to understand better. The implication was clear – they were seeking knowledge of the local inhabitants, and I was almost certainly next.

I buried my beast in the dust as best I could. In the big scheme of things, I really didn't begrudge the carcass to the indigenous wildlife, but it was important to show the shadows from beyond that we had some respect for life, even out here in the frontier zones.

That night I had thought the moonlight might keep them away, but it seemed that they had played me into a corner. I was awoken from my uneasy slumber by a loud crack of electricity, and a great flash lighting up the compound. I was awake in an instant and before I could even get to the window the implication was clear - they were trying to breach the wire! But no, in fact even this was a mere distraction, they were here. In my room! Two figures and a strange mechanical animal, struggling to get through my small doorway.

Still taking nothing for granted however, they held up their shields, lest I bring my

A is for Aliens

firearm to bear, as the metal beast advanced with unspeakable rapidity towards me. And there, in my own nightshirt and nothing else, it had me. Its grip was firm, yet light enough not to cause me permanent harm. A sharp scratch on my arm, from somewhere unseen, and my head went light, and a feeling of euphoria came over me. Oddly, before I lost consciousness completely, I felt as though I were glad that they were here. They had drugged me with something powerful that was, perhaps, also intended to be kind. My panic abated as I drifted into a deep sleep.

Abducted.

Gasping with fear I awoke on what I could only assume was their spaceship. Strong medicine continued to flow through my veins, perhaps from the strange tubes and surgical pumps all around. Once fully awake, my vision was oddly sharp and every detail seemed more real, brighter and more sharply focussed than anything I had witnessed before. The light was pinpoint clear and a true blue, unlike anything I had beheld previously. The temperature was warm and seemed designed to be as comforting to me as possible. There were metal tubes inserted in so many places I could not count, nor comprehend them all.

But it didn't seem to matter. There were voices, words perhaps, guttural sounds which must have meant something to them.

Despite the euphoria brought on by their foreign potions flowing in my veins, the vision of the, finally unsuited, aliens were utterly, utterly horrific to me. They had the same number of eyes, ears and limbs as us. But they were enormous, pink and flabby, everything bloated and coarse, where our flesh was smooth and greyer. Their little, hooded, slit-like, watery eyes observing me with rapt fascination and their disconcerting circle within a circle of their eyeballs made me feel utterly uncomfortable, despite their drugs, as though they could see into my soul.

I could feel my mind being washed clean, exactly as the out-of-towner had predicted. But I was made of tougher stuff. I determined that I would remember something clear and relatable despite their potions and brainwashing. So, I fixated on anything that might be memorable. I observed their imagery and hieroglyphics, some of which were repeated both large and small on clothing and other surfaces. Two things in particular I tried to fix in my mind, a strange graphic with darkly coloured suns and bars and also some, presumed, lettering. In my head I resolved to associate them with things I knew and could easily repeat. So, I created a mantra to remind myself and try to beat their attempts to erase my memory. A bucket, a serpent, and a trestle. I kept repeating to myself, holding the images hard in my mind's eye. Burning them into my memory. Bucket, serpent, trestle. Bucket, serpent, trestle.

I have no idea how long I was there. The whole thing is like the oddest, most beautiful, most disconcerting dream you ever experienced. When it was finally over, I awoke in my own unmade bed, supposedly to be convinced that nothing much had happened. But everything had happened. And that is when the authorities turned up.

Perhaps twenty or thirty riders arrived, all armed and dusty from hard riding. They fell on me, my cattle, and the whole homestead as if it was a nest of vipers that needed stamping to death.

A is for Aliens

I tried to tell them my story and the feelings of benevolence I had towards the aliens despite their evisceration of my animal and, in no small amount, my personal violations. But they would have nothing of it. I was mistaken. I was deluded. I needed to get a grip. I couldn't get a grip though. My life had changed forever. I had been taken by forces of which we knew nothing, against which we were powerless. Struggling was pointless. The aliens meant us no harm, they just wanted to understand, to help, to learn. Despite their utter foreignness to me, I had seen so much. Symbols and flags. Emblems and runes. Heard words and emotions, and they had talked to me somehow. Imprinting a sense of them into my brain. Ranting and railing, they dragged me away.

And that is how you find me now, delirious, incarcerated, but free at least from the aliens and their interventions. In a padded cell far from my former, remote life. Here I feel more liberated than you can truly understand, but my dreams are vexed. I often recall their odd insignia and strange alien writing. Particularly the large colourful image of stylised suns and bars, that seemed to adorn all the walls of their (truly I know it was) space craft.

But above all I remember their runes as I saw them so clearly repeated, the bucket, the serpent, and the trestle. My scheme had worked, I remember where so many others have forgotten. So always these memories haunt me, and I feel compelled to draw them and show them, warn others, and find some small consolation despite my perceived madness.

The bucket, the serpent, and the trestle. Bucket. Serpent. Trestle. Look, look! Let me draw them for you now...

U

S

A

See, see how strange they look!

Once again, the psychiatrist makes a note in her file and impatiently drums her three green fingers on the table. I pay her no heed; the aliens have spoken to me and I, nay we, will never be the same again.

To start with they only came at night.

Abducted

Astrid Addams

It started with the homeless. They began disappearing all over the city. One by one, the homeless that coloured the streets of Charlotte's city just vanished. They began to huddle together in anxious groups; Charlotte saw them whispering, speculating that the new government was taking them away, experimenting on them or sending them to some remote colony somewhere, or maybe just gassing them to save money. By the time the old man who sat in the subway, the one Charlotte always gave money to when she had change on her way to work, (she wouldn't normally but the man was old and haggard, with only one leg) disappeared, it was on the news. Homeless people disappearing all over the country and then the world. The hostels and homeless charities were empty, and no one seemed to know why.

World leaders and politicians in

designer suits argued in front of the world's media every night; it was clear all thought it was a good thing, one less problem to worry about. Even the politicians who claimed to be concerned and screamed for action, only did it to look good next to the opposition. Even Charlotte, who had never voted and believed all the monkeys in suits were the same, saw that. As did most people, so it seemed.

Then other people started to disappear. At first, one or two at a time, then whole streets and villages. Footage began appearing online of something large suddenly descending in the sky, blocking out the sun or the night stars. Charlotte and millions of others watched footage of the giant spaceships descend and flash a terrible poisonous green light. Arsenic-green, someone called it. Then the spaceship and all the people underneath would be gone. In some of the footage you could hear screams, cars crashing, guns firing. In one video Charlotte heard what appeared to be a bomb. But none of it made any difference, they'd still be gone with the green light.

Very little made it into the mainstream

media, except some of the mass suicides and child murders in villages and streets rumoured to have disappeared into the light. The riots and wars that raged as communities and countries combusted, oh yes that was reported. Absolutely nobody on television mentioned aliens, but that was all most people talked about online and in person, huddled together in groups on street corners and workplaces, Charlotte among them. Somehow being in a group felt safer.

After a year or so, the mass abductions seemed to stop, as far as anyone could tell, and the world seemed to hold its breath, hoping it was over. Hoping that whoever was in the spaceship big enough to cover whole towns had enough people for whatever purpose it desired, would just take them and go, leaving everyone else in peace. Charlotte and everyone else gradually started to relax. Over the next year, memorials were built to honor the missing and documentaries regularly appeared, speculating about the disappearances. Some blamed aliens, some serial killing cults, some global conspiracies and even gay marriage.

Charlotte turned 21 and started a new

job in an office nearer to home and started to date a man from her office who called her his pocket girl. He was 6ft and she was barely 5ft 2, so it sort of fitted. They were in the supermarket one Friday evening when it started again. Charlotte checked her phone as Jake got her a bottle of gin down from the shelf. It was a big enough story to make BBC news and this time it was only one person who had disappeared, but to Charlotte, suddenly, breathing air was like trying to breathe treacle. They had taken Ed Sheeran.

He was just the first. Other people disappeared, mainly under 40, attractive or talented singers, as if the aliens didn't care about being seen and had become more selective. At last, the politicians of the world admitted to the global problem and started to take steps to deal with it. Around the time Adele disappeared from her London home, Jake became controlling, dictating to Charlotte who she could talk to at work, what she could wear when she left the house, and what she could eat. By the time Beyoncé was snatched from the podium of an award ceremony, Jake was hitting her during their frequent screeching arguments, bearing down on her like a giant angry bear, taking out his own fear and helplessness on her small fragile body.

As riots raged across cities and the world combusted yet again, Jake's heavy drinking cost him his job and Charlotte could only leave the house in very heavy makeup. As Cher was reported missing by CNN, Jake sat on the edge of their bed and cried, begging Charlotte to forgive him as she lay naked in the middle of their bed, her body mottled with bruises, her face swelling beyond recognition, blood pumping from her broken nose and between her legs. Barely conscious she heard the news report and Jake's promise to change as he begged her not to leave him. She'd heard both before, and Cher being kidnapped by aliens was far more believable. The last thing she saw was the flash of arsenic green light and Jake's scream, as inevitable as the next punch, before the world turned black.

It was the sound of crying that woke Charlotte. Not a baby crying or weeping, no this was the howling sobs of someone just realising their worst nightmare had come true. Head and body throbbing, Charlotte opened her eyes as much as possible and understood why. She was in a white box with nothing but a toilet and a large water bottle with a small tap, twice her size, suspended from the ceiling. She was also naked under the soft blanket. One of the walls was just cage bars, reminding her of the box her parents took their cat to the vets in. Worse still, she remembered the green light and wondered why they had taken her and not Jake.

Then the crying stopped, and someone whined her name. Struggling to her feet, the blanket wrapped around her like a dress, she struggled forwards; he had really beat the shit out of her that time. Charlotte winced as she reached the small grill in the wall, he must have broken a rib again, the sanctimonious prick! She found herself face to face with Jake and felt a grim satisfaction.

"Charlotte, babe, thank God you're ok, you have to help me!" Jake sounded more frightened than Charlotte had ever heard him sound before.

"Where are we? What is this? Who are they?" Charlotte managed to gasp; breathing and talking were both painful in her current condition.

"I don't know, it's some sort of lab and

they're evil alien fucking giants. Seriously, they can hold us in their arms like we're cats or fucking lap dogs. You have to help me pocket girl, they cut my balls off.'

"Guess you won't be fucking the shit out of me again any time soon then." Satisfaction filtered through Charlotte's haze as she felt around her mouth, wondering if any teeth were missing or loose.

"They took the guy away next door to me and they haven't brought him back yet. It's been hours, or days, I don't know. You have to help me. Pocket Lottie? Where you going?"

Ignoring Jake's self-pity and ranting, Charlotte made the short painful walk to the bars of her crate and peered out.

They were in a room so large it resembled a universe. It was clean and light and across from them, about the length of about a football pitch, were other bars which Charlotte speculated must be a skyscraper of crates. She wondered if Ed Sheeran was in one. Charlotte leaned forwards, her head fitting easily through the bars, and she was able to peer lengthways down the room. That's when she saw it and felt the need to curl up and tremble as close to Jake as she could get.

Violent and controlling he may be, but at least he was familiar. Right now, staring helplessly at the green mountain that seemed to glide and pulsate at the end of the room, she wanted familiarity more than anything else. It, whatever it was, was a terrible poisonous green, the same green as the light that people had been disappearing into, never to be seen again.

A sick feeling crept into her body, scuttling through her veins like tiny insects as she watched the mountain glide slowly in her direction. She thought of her mum and dad and her friends. She hadn't seen her friends in months in a futile attempt to appease Jake's rampant jealousy. She hadn't seen her mum and dad in weeks because Jake didn't like her to. How her heart ached for her family and friends now, and how much she hated the whining, sobbing, self-centred wreck next door. If they had to take her, she wished they had taken her with anyone else other than this prick. Tears started to stream down her face. What the hell was the green blob doing beside the cages? Her eyes ached as she looked at it and suddenly her stomach turned. Charlotte found herself stumbling to the toilet and vomiting herself dry.

A gentle but unpleasant touch at the back of her shoulders sent her wheeling around with a squawk to find a long green pulsing tentacle reaching for her through the now open door. In a state of panic, she did everything she could in the tiny space to dodge the fast-moving appendage. Trying to jump over, it she tripped and fell with a scream. The tentacle gripped her in mid-air, causing a stabbing pain in her backside before everything went black. Later she awoke, back up in her cage, to discover food - some sort of unnatural biscuits in a bowl. The smell of something chemical lingered on her skin which tingled and ached still, but there was nothing to suggest further injury yet.

Determinedly, she ignored Jake and his pleas and ate a couple of biscuits. They tasted okay and she hadn't realised how long it had been since she'd last eaten. Eventually, Jake shut up and Charlotte was able to get some sleep.

Without any means of telling the time, and no apparent night or day in the room outside, the hours and days dragged on indefinitely. She slept when she was tired, ate and drank when she was hungry and thirsty, and tried to block out the screams of the people in the crates around her. As the bruises began to fade and her aching body mend, she became restless and began running in circles around the crate. Most of all she tried to block out Jake, who mainly seemed to alternate between sobbing and raging.

Every so often, one of the greens would glide into the room and replace the biscuits. When this happened, she'd peer through the bars at the pulsating green flesh that seemed to move and ripple even when it stood still. As she stared, she noticed small continuous colour changes through the ripples and wondered what lived beneath the terrible green.

Other times the creature would come into the sterile white, a sleeping person entwined in its tentacles, sometimes clutched to the pulsing green slime of its belly. Each time, Charlotte was convinced the belly would absorb the sleeping person, and each time she'd be wrong and the tentacles would place the sleeping form into a crate. Sometimes people were taken from the crates. If Charlotte heard screams, the screams would stop suddenly and they'd be limp in the monsters' tentacles. If they didn't scream or fight, they'd be lifted out upright in the tentacles and peered at closely. Charlotte had never seen any eyes but that's what it was doing. She could feel it in her own flesh. Then the person was carted away, just as the unconscious ones were. Sometimes they'd be returned to their crates, other times they'd never come back and Charlotte's own screams and sobs would join the symphony of Jake and the others.

Jake was taken away four times, each time kicking and screaming before being returned unharmed each time. It was the only time she spoke to him, to ask him what had happened, but he was never able to tell her. However, he was beginning to get over his initial terror. She could feel it as he battered the walls and swore vengeance on her and the universe and 'those green fuckers'. When he was taken away for the fifth time he never came back, and Charlotte sobbed and prayed and mourned for the loss of the one reminder of her old life, the one link with her family and friends back home on Earth. They weren't on Earth; she could feel it in her bones and hear it in the constant white noise that rattled from the vents and supplied the oxygen. Charlotte swore that the next time she was taken, she would not scream or fight and would see what was beyond the God-like doors Jake had never returned from.

When the green tentacle reached into her bare home for the third time, she steeled herself and thought of the kitten her parents had bought her as a girl and the first time they took it to the vet. How it had just hung in the vet's large hand, wide-eyed and crying. The tentacles wrapped around her, tightening gently around her flesh. Charlotte felt a wave of cold, goose bumps popping out all over her skin as she sank slightly into the terrible green flesh as if she was being kidnapped by a bouncy castle. The tentacles lifted her into the air and Charlotte bit her lip to stop herself screaming. Then she was out of the cage, trying not to look down, knowing that she was suspended from what felt like the same height as the Empire State Building, where she'd stood as a child. Looking down, the world had seemed to spin, and she'd asked to go back down. This time, as then, she forced her eyes to look out at the surrounding area and what had to be the head of the green.

It was not easily identifiable as a head, in that there was no neck and it had no obvious features. Instead, Charlotte was held up to a green flat rippling surface so shiny she could see herself reflected in it. As she stared at her reflection, she noticed how long her brown hair had got and how much weight she had gained since Jake no longer controlled her diet. Charlotte saw something swim to the surface of whatever green slime the creature was comprised of. Something black and large and round kept swimming closer towards the surface, getting bigger and bigger before breaking through the slime. The bulging blank sphere peered at Charlotte, and soon it was followed by another, then another, until a total of four eyes had burst through the thing's flesh and bulged at her, reflecting her in every single one.

Suddenly, the thing lowered her onto a silver metal-like surface. She'd been too engrossed in the weird eyeballs to notice they had been gliding out of the room and into another, where an almost identical bulging green stood. It was taller and slightly wider and the larger green glided closer to the table as tentacles emerged from its bulky form. A large tentacle seized the edge of her blanket and yanked it from her form. She yelped at the sudden exposure, mortified, using her hands and arms to cover herself as best she could. They may be about as human as the glitter slim poos sold on Earth, but it was her body, God damn it, and she hated them looking at it.

It did not stop with a quick look, the taller and fatter green examining her from every possible angle. To examine her teeth, it held long prongs in its tentacles and carefully examined with far more gentleness and dexterity than her own dentist. Clean metal prongs of different shapes and textures were used to examine her internally. Held firmly in place, and gritting her teeth as she felt the cold metal slide into her anus, Charlotte prayed that Flubber's giant brother would not make any mistakes. After what felt like forever, samples had been scraped from her vaginal walls and she was finally given back the blanket and carried from the room. Not back into the room she had just come from, but into another gloriously white room where she was handed over to another blob and put into a carry case before being carried down a long corridor. Pressed to the bars, she looked desperately at the white corridor for anything stimulating or of interest but, to her despair, she found nothing.

The stableness of the crate told her that she was clutched against the bulk of the creature. As they neared the end, the thing stopped, and tentacles penetrated the bars until they found her. Charlotte clung to the bars of the cage trembling, tears pouring down her face. The pain in her rump told her that she was soon going to be unconscious again. Just as they reached what appeared to be a giant glass cube, the world went black.

***

When she came to, Charlotte found herself lying in the crate. Trembling, and with a terrible sick feeling, she got to her feet and looked towards the barred door. It was open and, for a long time, Charlotte just stared at the door. Every anxiety she'd had since she'd been taken playing matinees in quick succession through her

A is for Aliens

mind. Charlotte had never wanted her mum so badly in her life before and cursed Jake yet again. Since their abduction he had become the focus of all her hate and anger at her situation. Charlotte didn't care if it was fair or not, but the thought that he might be out there waiting for her without a wall between them carried her to the doorway and cautiously through. After all, she had a score to settle.

What she found outside was not Jake however, but a vast white room with odd grey shapes that seemed to have some sort of purpose, although she wasn't sure what that might be. When she stepped on the floor, she found it to be thick, grass-like carpet that covered her knees and probably tickled the bottom of the greens who glided by. Looking around the plain room, Charlotte was relieved to find no green but a food bowl and water bottle against the nearest wall.

"Morning sleepy head."

Charlotte let out a cry and jumped back, the gravelly male voice was somehow horrific in the pure white. Looking around frantically as the man's laugh rang out, she couldn't see the him nor anyone else.

A is for Aliens

"Down here love." A familiar face popped out of the long carpet and grinned at her. Charlotte screamed.

It took a while, but Charlotte was starting to settle into her new home. Well, to the extent that she no longer needed what she assumed were laxatives to use the exposed toilet. It was hard to tell how long she had been there; sitting on the windowsill, looking out at the grey world she learnt that it was never night. Always a cream, a couple of shades less bright than the house's interior except when it stormed. Then rain would pelt the ground as if it was a hammer and the sky would turn concrete grey. She spent a long time on the windowsill, looking at the ever oozing and streaming life outside. They all did; it was their only contact with the outside world.

The green also owned two other people. The first was the man with the gravelly voice who insisted on being called Whacko Jacko and refused to wear anything but a cap and a robotic leg. She had known him on Earth, well, she passed him on the street and occasionally gave him change on her way to work. He'd been cleaner shaved then; now he appeared to be growing a giant carpet. Looking at the spine that poked through his skin and the exposed collar bones, Charlotte felt an enormous sense of guilt that she had never lifted a finger to help him beyond a few coins. To compound her guilt, the man, neutered like Jake had been, was never anything but kind to her and Trix.

Trix was the other woman. She told Charlotte her entire street had been taken in the first mass abduction. She was slightly older than Charlotte and had blonde hair, blue eyes, and a number of tattoos and piercings. She was also about Charlotte's height, which was a rarity in itself. The woman insisted on being called Trix after the Siamese cat she'd owned on Earth. After all, that's what they were in this alien world.

The green had given them a giant bed, not much different to an Earth bed, a decent imitation which Charlotte and Trix slept at opposite ends of. Whacko slept on the greens furniture or embedded in the carpet. Charlotte and Trix had brilliantly coloured dresses to wear and Charlotte made sure she always wore one. The Whacko refused to touch any clothes so Trix tended to wear the suits, shirts, and ties meant for him. The green occasionally left them toys, beach balls, skipping ropes, art supplies, and the odd book. Whacko, with a grin, informed them that the greens must be working towards higher animal welfare standards as they tossed the beach ball to each other. Whacko was definitely the green's favourite - every so often it would pick him up and sit him on its green belly, run it tentacles down his back and over his knobbly spine and coo. It never seemed to want to do that with Charlotte or Trix and both were perfectly happy with that.

As the time passed, the three got to know one another better and Charlotte's nerves were not eased by what she found out.

"You must be a baby machine like me," Trix had said, at least seven months pregnant and rubbing her belly. "This will be the third space baby."

Charlotte had looked dubiously at Wacko who was scratching a scar on his chest. Trix laughed a humourless laugh.

"No, that fucker brings men here and locks me in a crate with them. If we don't do it, we won't get let out of the crate and we won't get the biscuits. It's best to just get it over with, then they feed you, but you'll be stuck in that crate to fuck until your knocked up."

"Where are the babies?" Charlotte asked, a knot of anxiety gnawing at her insides.

Trix shrugged her shoulders and bit her lip.

"When it's time to deliver them they take me away, knock me out with whatever shit they inject in your butt, and take the baby out of me. First time I woke up with no baby. The last one, a boy, was taken a while back now. I cried buckets but hopefully he's gone to a loving home." They both shuddered at the words.

"That green fucker will want to breed you too, you know." Trix warned as they tried to sleep. Trix's words kept Charlotte from sleeping long after her companions started snoring.

A while later, after Trix had returned with a tiny baby girl and sat nursing her, Charlotte asked a question which had been playing on her mind.

"Hey, why did they neuter him?" Charlotte pointed at Whacko, sleeping within the carpet. "If they want to breed from us?"

"God knows," Trix shrugged. "Let's wake him and ask; he sleeps all the time anyway. I wish this one slept as much."

It took them a good few nudges to wake their sleeping companion, but eventually he stirred and greeted them with his usual good humour.

"Charlotte wants to know why those green fuckers cut your balls off," Trix said, once the old man had stopped coughing. Whacko's coughs turned to wheezing laughter.

"Well I don't know for sure," he wheezed eventually, "but I always thought it was on account of me being a rampaging piss-head who could pick a fight with a letter box if I didn't like how it looked at me. They probably don't want to be filling their water bottles with Special Brew and trying to get the piss and puke out their posh carpets."

"But you're one of the sweetest men ever, you're not aggressive at all," said Charlotte, remembering Jake.

"I might be without the booze and testosterone or whatever was rushing through my veins. It don't always work, mind, a friend of mine who'd been big into his drugs went to pieces after they cut his nuts off. Practically tried to eat his way through the bars he did, before they took him away and put him to sleep like we did with dogs on Earth."

"Why keep people they can't breed from?" asked Trix, paler than usual, clutching her baby tightly.

"Ah well, I reckon they're breeding you lovely ladies for pretty little pets and, whilst I can't reproduce, I can be a pet our green owner had the satisfaction of saving and giving a better life to. What you ladies produce will probably be the green equivalent of Chihuahua's and Shih Tzu's. I'm the scared rescue dog kept from the lethal injection."

As time passed, Trix's baby grew bigger and more independent as Whacko grew weaker. His appetite was vanishing, his already stooped, skeletal frame became almost translucent, and his robotic leg had to be adjusted as his stump shrank. The mostly absent green became a much more involved feature of their lives, holding Whacko Jacko on its belly, tentacles wrapped around him. Every time Whacko was placed in the carry case and taken away Charlotte was convinced that he would not be returning.

One particularly stormy day, when the rain hammered the roof of whatever structure sheltered them, Charlotte and Trix huddled around the hysterical baby. The carry case returned empty and the green swept them all up in its tentacles and pushed them against, and into, its cold quivering slime. Later, when dishing out the usual biscuits, they found a new pellet mixed in. Charlotte picked it up, sniffed it, and gave it a small nibble. It was the nicest thing she had tasted since she had left Earth. Eagerly, she invited Trix to try the new food and, taking a bite, Trix's face lit up.

"Mmm, I could live on this," Trix mumbled through her full mouth as they tucked into the new food. The green also seemed to like this new food, eating it from a giant dish, scooping the pellets into a hole that appeared in its slime.

When the baby was able to crawl, another green came to the house and took it away in a tiny carry case. Trix screamed and cried, locked away with Charlotte as they watched through the bars. Charlotte had never felt so helpless as she held her friend and wished that she could ease her suffering. After losing her third baby, Trix became much quieter and Charlotte desperately missed the old Trix, as well as Whacko. The only thing that seemed to make things better for both of them was the new food, which the green dispensed every so often.

One day, whilst Trix slept on the bed and the green was nowhere in sight, Charlotte decided to leave the room to steal some of the special food. It felt like a week since they'd had any and Trix seemed to be becoming more depressed.

The special food would perk her up; she'd just have to hope the green did not notice.

It was a long journey through the thick carpet towards the giant door the green had carelessly left open. She had to stop and rest a number of times but finally she made it. Creeping through the door, Charlotte found herself on a hard, smooth floor. Looking up, she found it to be a high room with lots of grey shapes. Searching for a way to get higher up, she found what appeared to be a high barred tower next to a wall. Slowly and carefully she began to climb it, thoughts of the special food and Trix's face lighting up again kept her climbing.

A is for Aliens

After what felt like hours, Charlotte finally found herself at the top of a metal table. Staring into the milky dead eyes of Whacko, the only thing that stopped her from falling to her death was the clenching of her fingers in shock. Wacko's severed head, along with other body parts, were arranged in a line on the table and sick rose into Charlotte's mouth. The body parts looked dried out and preserved by something. Bits of Whacko's flesh were being moulded into the shape of the special food that both her and Trix loved. The one thing that made Trix happy was the compressed flesh and bones of Whacko, the man who had been kind enough to babysit so she and Trix could sleep. The man who had been the greens favourite. Was this to be their fate too?

A noise from outside startled Charlotte into looking up and she peered out the window next to the tower. The world outside was grey but was no longer boring. Instead, what Charlotte faced was a medieval artist's depiction of hell. Green's glided by as people were roasted golden brown on spits and seemed to disappear into green holes. Strange combinations of creature's, part human and insectoid, walked alongside their greens on leashes. Hanging, facing her, were people in giant cages. Forced to sing for the entertainment of the greens as dead babies were devoured from packets like chocolate bars.

Some greens were no longer just greens; she saw one with a shark's head stuck uncomfortably on its arsenic-green slim as it listened to one of the singers in the bird cage. People hung upside down in windows like carcasses in a butcher's shop, some without skin. Some greens carried cases or bags with people peering over the edge.

Charlotte didn't remember the journey down the tower. One minute she was watching a human head being used as a squeaky toy by a grasshopper with two human legs. Next, she was back in the grass-like carpet, wading towards her water dispenser, gulping down water, and rinsing her face. Charlotte realized she was trembling.

At the bed she found Trix under the sheets, still asleep. Charlotte curled up beside Trix and clung to her until the trembling subsided and she eventually went to sleep. She dreamt of Whacko, except Whacko's head was now attached to the body of an old mongrel that licked her face. In the bed with them she felt his presence and cried. When they woke up, Charlotte did not mention what she'd seen. She spent time with the green who owned them whenever she could, and the green's tentacles wound in her hair and caressed her back. When a small man was brought around, and she was placed in his carry case, she didn't complain. After all she was lucky, they were lucky.

Buddy

Lesley Drane

I'd just turned a page in *Harry Potter and the Chamber of Secrets* when my dog suddenly shot across the room, pulling me out of Harry Potter's world and back to reality.

"Really, Sophie?" I groaned as she barked furiously at whatever she could see through the window. It was 10pm on New Year's Eve 2019, the start of a new decade imminent, and all I wanted to end the year with was some peace and quiet. With a sharp bark, Sophie turned and sped off towards the back door. Sighing, I put down my book and followed.

Once I reached the door, she was already there pacing and growling. Probably just the neighbour's cat waiting on the wall to wind her up again, I thought to myself. "Okay, Sophie, just a minute!" I said as I unlocked the door and opened it.

As soon as the gap was big enough to squeeze through, Sophie shot through the opening and stopped. Wondering what had attracted her attention, I opened the door wider to see what Sophie was sniffing at. There seemed to be a large beach ball on the decking... except it couldn't be a beach ball as it was luminous and glowing. Sophie lifted her paw; I could see that she was about to give it a push. Shooing her away, I stared at the object as it slowly started to spin, spewing blues and greens across the garden wall. Where had it come from? I was tempted to reach out and touch it but didn't know for sure if it was safe to do so, plus I was respectful of having eight fingers and two thumbs. My digits might be arthritic, but I would still prefer to keep them intact.

The sphere stopped spinning, shuddered to a halt, and let out a loud burp. "Pardon you," I said, starting to feel bemused by this strange ball. Sophie was now growling further down the garden, most likely at the cat. Now still and silent, an aperture opened in the sphere and out stepped a figure.

Standing at what I'd assume to be only six inches high, the figure looked up at me with huge green eyes. It had broad shoulders, narrow hips and waist, plus a tiny nose and blue lips. It was suited up in bright purple with matching boots and gloves. It looked like it could possibly be a male extra-terrestrial, not that I would really know what one looks like. The little being started to shiver and I immediately felt sorry for it.

"Hi there, Buddy, you look cold." I leant down and held my palm out flat, the figure immediately taking hold of my finger and stepping up onto my hand. I brought myself back up slowly, trying to keep my hand as steady as possible.

Leaving the door open for the dog, I turned, heading for the warmth of the house. I grabbed a tea towel from the hall radiator and wrapped it around his shoulders. He immediately stopped shivering, seemingly grateful for the heat.

Walking back into the lounge, I sat on the sofa and placed the stranger on the coffee table.

"Well, Buddy, where did you come from? Are you ok? Hungry? Do you have a name?" All the questions that had been running through my mind were now slipping straight out of my mouth. He regarded me with his big green eyes.

"My name is Buddy. I do believe that is what you called me, yes?" Buddy turned and let the tea towel fall off his shoulders. He surveyed the room before swivelling back towards me. "And you are?" he asked.

Amazed that he could speak English, I

was silent for a moment. "I only called you Buddy as I didn't know what else to call you. I am called Amelia, though Amy will suffice."

"Ameeeeliaaa. That is a pretty name. I will call you Ameeeliaaa. May I sit by you? I feel awkward standing here."

I held my hand out towards Buddy who took my fingers and stepped back onto it. I placed him on the cushion next to me before turning my worry to Sophie—she was likely to come back in soon as she could be heard in the kitchen, licking her empty food bowl. In a minute, she would toss it across the floor as a hint that it needed refilling. I wasn't too sure how she would react to this strange being on the sofa. Sophie would either try to lick Buddy or would bark and frighten him. Another part of me was concerned that she would eat him.

As if reading my thoughts, Buddy asked, "Who or what is making those clanking and banging sounds?"

"Oh, that's my dog Sophie. But don't worry, I won't let her hurt you." Buddy didn't look very convinced and I must admit that I didn't either!

"I can't keep calling you Buddy, what's your real name?" I asked the being. He was busy removing his boots and gloves,

A is for Aliens

revealing bright purple socks and vibrant purple hands with six fingers on each. It seemed that this little alien was my favourite colour!

"My name is 457092419201346, though Buddy will suffice; I quite like it." Buddy grinned at me, showing a very wide mouth filled with sharp, pointed teeth—they weren't purple, but not quite white either. Resisting the urge to say, 'What sharp teeth you have,' I grinned back.

Buddy reached out and took my hand in both of his, turning it over to inspect it. "Your hand is very bony, and what are these curious lumps and bumps on it? Are they painful?"

"Those lumps and bumps are arthritis and yes they are quite painful. Though I guess you wouldn't know what arthritis is." Buddy slowly let go of my hand and, after a moment of silence, I changed the subject. "Anyway, where have you come from and are there any more like you in the sphere outside?"

Buddy looked in the direction of the door, towards where you could now hear the dog's claws tapping on the wooden floor of the hall as she headed back to the warmth of the lounge and her favourite spot on the sofa. Buddy stepped off the cushion, rushing towards the safety of my hands, terror in his eyes. I picked him up and placed him on the arm of the sofa where Sophie wouldn't see him. "Thank you," he whispered as the dog bounded in, leapt onto the settee and settled down to sleep.

"That's ok, I told you that you would be safe."

Starting to relax, Buddy sat cross-legged on the soft leather and began to tell me his story.

***

"I was flying my craft when the directional controls malfunctioned. I missed the black hole that I was headed for and my craft got caught in the gravitational pull of your planet. I tried to steer my ship towards a safe place and ended up landing in your garden. I was the only one in my craft. There were other ships in front of me heading back to my home. No one saw me lose control. I don't expect they will come looking for me as they won't know where or when I disappeared." Buddy gave a big sigh. "I am afraid that you are stuck with me for now, until I get my craft fixed. That is if I can fix it."

"You are welcome here, Buddy,

although it will get quite noisy soon. The neighbours will be setting light to fireworks as we set off into the New Year and a new decade. I doubt you know what that means?" Buddy's face remained blank so I continued on, "I will switch on the television and show you. Fireworks are amazing, but as I said, very loud, flashy, and bright."

Buddy told me that he knew a lot about Earth, that they studied our planet and our customs, which was why he could speak English. "I am looking forward to seeing these fireworks you speak of—we don't have those on our planet."

"Why is Earth so interesting to you? Surely there are other inhabited planets. I mean, you come from one for a start, and you have no problem breathing our air; you weren't even wearing a helmet."

"We love your planet and its fauna. Earth is extremely old; much older than our planet, and as to your air, it is the same as ours, except we have no pollution, no vehicles or manufacturing to spoil ours. In time, your planet will be destroyed by yourselves, no alien invasion to worry about. In fact, our planet could be your new home if you had the technology to build spaceships that could navigate and survive the journey to ours.

My home is a long way from here, it would take a hundred Earth years to reach us. We can do the journey in minutes; Earth minutes, that is. We don't have time in the way you do."

Buddy inspected his hands; I didn't quite catch the look that passed across his features. I was enthralled by this little alien and didn't view him as a threat.

"So, Buddy, what's your plan? Do you need to rest, or do you wish to return to your spaceship to start repairs?"

Buddy looked up at me. "I will stay here for now, if I may, and watch these fireworks you mentioned. Then I will return to my ship and see if I can summon help. There might be other craft in the vicinity that could hear my distress signal."

I reached for the remote and switched the television on. There was still a while to wait before Big Ben would strike the hour of midnight whence the fireworks would begin. "You have time to send that signal, there is still over an hour to go yet. I can call you when midnight is near."

Buddy looked over at the television that was now on. "Hmmm, you speak of an Earth hour, we don't have this, so yes, please call me. Will you return me to my ship now, please?"

A is for Aliens

I passed him his boots and gloves and, after he had put them on, I reached out my hand and Buddy hopped onto my palm. I stood up and walked to the back of the house, pushed open the door and placed him gently onto the decking. Buddy approached the ball and pressed his hand against it, whereupon an aperture appeared. Buddy turned to me.

"If you just knock, I will come back out." With that, he stepped into the doorway of the craft and the opening closed behind him.

***

I returned to the lounge, sat back on the sofa and contemplated. Was the alien as friendly as he seemed? Had he arrived by accident or design? Was it safe to let him back in? So many questions and I had no idea what the answers were. I didn't even know what he ate or whether he slept.

I debated whether to let Buddy back in. He wouldn't know if an hour had passed. I could just pretend that I fell asleep and then check in the morning to see whether the strange sphere was still there. As I struggled with these conflicting thoughts, I realised that not letting him back in would indicate that I didn't trust him. I could be perceived as a threat, rather than the opposite way around. Oh, decisions!

As there was still plenty of time, I got up and retrieved Sophie's lead from the hall, along with my jacket, and called her. I didn't want her going out the back whilst the alien spaceship was still sat on the decking, especially as Sophie had already shown an interest in it. I put my jacket on, clipped on her lead and headed out into the cold, crisp evening air, hoping it might clear my head.

At five minutes to midnight, I made my way to the back of the house, opened the back door and knocked on the sphere. The entrance opened and out stepped Buddy.

"Any luck?" I asked the alien, as I returned with him to the lounge and the television for us to watch the fireworks.

"I don't know yet. I will return to my craft after seeing these fireworks and spend the remaining hours of darkness there working on repairs." He was sat on the arm of the sofa again, but this time waiting for the countdown to begin.

The hands of Big Ben landed on the twelve and the crowds cheered as the fireworks began. They were spectacular and Buddy was enthralled.

I answered my mobile as my daughter rang to wish me Happy New Year. Buddy studied my phone as I put it down. "Does that work off the satellites?" he asked.

"No, from cell phone towers," I replied. "Do you have any communication devices on your planet? A way to speak to others? I really don't know that much about you or your planet." I looked at Buddy for answers, trying to determine whether this six-inch being was a threat to humanity or just lost and harmless. I chastised myself silently. I shouldn't watch so many sci-fi films!

Buddy gave me another of his wide, sharp-toothed grins. "Does your dog usually make that strange noise?" He nodded towards Sophie who was snoring away loudly. "And what is the point of the animal? It only seems to make a lot of racket." He suddenly started to shake and made a weird sound himself. I realised that he was laughing, and also neatly evading my questions.

"Sophie eats, sleeps, and farts. She also likes to chase the neighbour's cat. But you still haven't said anything about you or your planet. Where were you coming from when you crash-landed?" I regarded Buddy, who was making himself comfortable again by removing his boots and gloves. He obviously wasn't in a rush to return to his spacecraft to fix it or try to make contact with his peers.

Buddy looked up from taking off his gloves, his huge green eyes looking innocent. With a sigh, he said that it would be difficult for him to explain or answer any of my questions. "You would really need to see my planet to understand, Ameeeliaaa. It would be like me trying to describe Earth to my friends who have never been here. We have things that I wouldn't know how to explain to you. As to where I had been, we were visiting a planet over two solar systems away from here, the only route there via various black holes; the planet was dying, and we went to assist." Buddy didn't seem to want to explain as to how they were going to assist. Help the planet to die or survive? I wasn't sure that I wanted to know.

"Did it work—the assistance? Was there life to be saved or just an uninhabited planet?"

Buddy tilted his head, considering my questions. "May I have some water, please, not from your tap, but from the fridge? Also, some melted ice with it too? It is quite warm in here. If you want me to carry on talking, I need a drink first—my mouth is thirsty."

Checking that Sophie was still asleep, I

A is for Aliens

got up, walked to the kitchen, and grabbed a knife and bowl from the drainer. I opened the freezer and scraped some ice into the bowl before finding a shot glass and spooning some of the ice from the bowl into it. I then put the glass in the microwave, turned the dial to five seconds and pressed the start button. Once it dinged, I opened the microwave and checked the glass; the ice had melted and was still cool.

I returned to the lounge and handed the small glass to Buddy. As his hands touched the cold glass, they turned blue. He hastily took a few sips from it before handing it back. As the glass left his hands, they returned to their usual purple colour—he obviously wasn't too comfortable with being cold.

"The planet was dying, as I told you. No sustainable life left on there, not that we could have helped. We were there to make sure the planet didn't cause a problem to the rest of the solar system it resided in. We made sure it imploded. Had it exploded, the shockwaves would have travelled through the black holes which sometimes destroys them. That curtails our travels so we can't allow that. There is also the problem of Earth's plastic which is starting to block the black holes too.

A is for Aliens

This cannot be allowed to carry on. As your planet continues to cause a problem to the rest of your solar system, we will need to do the same here." He stops and looks at me, waiting for a response, but I don't have one. "Ameeeliaaa? Are you ok?"

I was dumbstruck; here was an alien, sat on my sofa arm, telling me about the future of my home, my planet. Were we next? Was Earth going to be destroyed by six-inch aliens? Dare I ask as to when that might be?

Buddy stretched his body. His mouth opened very wide as he yawned, exposing a lot more of his sharp teeth, teeth that could rip something to shreds. Containing a shudder, I told myself not to be so stupid—he'd had plenty of chances to bite my fingers off, and he didn't want to harm me, only my planet. Same difference though.

"Ameeeliaaa, don't look so shocked, your Earth is dying anyway. As I have said before, we don't have time on my planet, not the way it is measured here. I can't answer your question just yet."

I stuttered, "I, er, didn't ask you a question."

Buddy held out his hand to me. "Your expression said enough. Please don't be afraid of me. I am very tired though; may I sleep in your warm house tonight? The spacecraft is colder than I thought."

***

I realised that I was still holding the glass that Buddy had given back to me. "Do you want some more water or anything to eat? I'm not sure where you could sleep here, let me have a think. You need a safe place, away from Sophie." I realised that I was rambling, but I wanted to know more. Was he really here by accident? I had seen a beach ball in my garden back in the summer, thought it had been blown in there by the wind. A couple of days later it had disappeared; another windy day had carried it elsewhere, or so I had surmised. "Were you here last year? Your craft looks very similar to something that was in my garden before, in our summer."

Buddy, stifling yet another yawn, looked shifty. "Umm, yes, I might have been. I thought I recognised the dog. I was checking to see if you humans were still making your plastics. May I sleep now? We can continue this conversation when I have slept."

"Just a few more minutes, Buddy, then I will find somewhere safe for you. I have one more question... well, two actually. Who made the decision about imploding Earth? And how long have we got?"

Buddy stretched and another yawn strained his mouth even wider. I wondered who would fare the worst should Sophie decide he was a delicacy to eat. "Well, um, that would be me, but until my communication device is working, I can't organise the crew that does the job. But you needn't worry, Ameeeliaaa, I have already told you that you can return with me to my planet. You will be safe there."

Sighing, I got up. "Okay, Buddy, I can see that you are shattered and need to sleep. I will be back shortly. I'm sure I have something that you can sleep in." Leaving the lounge, I went to the kitchen cupboard where I had a small shortbread tin left over from Christmas. If I put some bubble wrap inside, it would keep him safe and warm, enveloped in plastic. Oh, the irony!

I returned from the kitchen with the tin. It had a lid that snapped on, but I had left that bit behind—didn't want to starve the alien of oxygen. I picked Buddy up and popped him in. "Is that okay for you? Comfortable? You can sleep in there and I will put the tin on the dining table."

Buddy looked up from where he was

now resting, snuggled into the bubble wrap, and closed his eyes. "Perfect," he mumbled and promptly fell asleep. I moved the biscuit tin to the dining table, then went into the hall and got my coat and Sophie's lead. Her last walk before I retired to bed, plus I could think without worrying that my thoughts might be heard.

***

I smoked whilst we walked. I had a plan in mind and my thought processes always seemed to work far better with the help of nicotine and fresh air. I smiled as we strolled, Sophie enjoying the exercise, and I was sure that my idea would be a satisfactory solution. I really couldn't see how I could possibly fit in the alien's spacecraft, for starters. I would be lucky if my hand fit, let alone the rest of me. Besides, I was not about to leave my kids and mum behind, and then there was Sophie. She would be in her element chasing little aliens though. I chuckled at that thought.

I let us both in through the front door, being as quiet as I could. I unclipped Sophie's lead, hung up my coat, and followed her into the kitchen where she'd

A is for Aliens

always wait for her evening treat. I gave her a few gravy bones from the box which she scoffed down. After waiting to see if there were any more, and realising that there weren't, she went into the lounge and settled back on the settee. It wasn't long before she was asleep, her front leg twitching as she chased something in her dreams.

I followed silently behind. I had left the lights on, but that hadn't bothered Buddy. Saliva bubbles escaped his lips as he exhaled. He was out for the count. I gently picked up the tin and returned to the kitchen, placing the tin on the counter. Buddy didn't stir. I picked up the lid to the shortbread tin and quietly pushed it down, sealing it. Opening the freezer door, I placed Buddy inside and pushed the door closed.

Part one of the plan in place, I locked up and switched off the lights. As I made my way to bed, I hoped that Buddy would freeze while asleep. My plan certainly didn't include him chewing his way out! I set my alarm for seven a.m. I didn't want to sleep too long; I needed to be up early.

My alarm beeped noisily seemingly only seconds after I had closed my eyes. I hurriedly got dressed and headed to the kitchen where I switched the kettle on. A mug of coffee before part two. The freezer door was still shut tight. I had no intention of checking on Buddy just yet. My plan would only work if he was frozen enough to prevent him from using his many teeth. I felt terrible, but survival of the fittest depended on it.

I made my coffee, switching the kettle off just before it boiled, still trying to be quiet. I took my coffee into the lounge and used my mobile phone to check the internet for the information I wanted.

I enjoyed a cigarette whilst sipping my coffee, checking my watch a couple of times. I didn't turn the television on as I usually would, and Sophie didn't stir. Putting my mug on the coffee table, I returned to the kitchen and got a black rubbish bag from under the sink, unlocked the back door and ventured outside. The sphere was still there, still resembling a beach ball. Grabbing my gardening gloves, I upended the black bag over the ball and tipped it in.

Afterwards, I went to the freezer. I could see that the shortbread tin still had its lid in place with no sign of holes in the tin. I quickly plucked it out of the freezer and placed it inside the black bag too. I tied the bag tight and headed out the front door.

A is for Aliens

The binmen were due soon. It was unusual for them to be working New Year's Day, but also lucky for me that they were. I saw the bin lorry turn in to my road and waited for it. My heart was beating fast and my hands were trembling. One of the men hopped out of the lorry as it pulled up, took the bag from me and chucked it into the back. I watched as the steel jaws crunched down on the black bag. "Happy New Year!" I grinned at the young man, and under my breath said, "And good riddance to bad rubbish!"

Pike Street

Monster Smith

I

It was a beautiful, cool day out, the perfect temperature as Kurt Bigelow stepped into the sunlight, letting it bathe over him. He'd been anxiously anticipating this moment for weeks and was fully prepared for fun that awaited him. School was out for the next three months, and today marked the first day of their traditional summer break.

Jimmy Lentz and a few other neighborhood boys were walking up the path toward Kurt, passing a ball back and forth. As they approached, Sean Huncomb quickly snatched the ball out of Jimmy's hands and flung it at Kurt.

"Heads up," said Sean with a big grin, ecstatic that he managed to catch Kurt off guard.

Kurt had turned thirteen a couple days earlier and thought of the break as a delayed birthday present to himself. It was his favorite time of the year; no school,

A is for Aliens

with nothing to do over the next few months but have fun. He had no bedtime and spent every waking hour outside, seeing what he and his friends could get themselves into.

At the end of the block, Kurt noticed Ham and his group of thugs bullying a younger girl from their school. Her name was Kelly Ann Garris, the prettiest girl in class. As much as he wanted to, he knew better than to mess with Ham and his friends...it never ended well for those who did. Besides, he figured Ham had a crush on Kelly Ann, the same as every other boy in town.

"We're going to hit the courts," said Jeff. "You coming with?"

Jeff Leer was that athletic friend that everyone had, always trying his best to convince people to hit the courts or do some other strenuous activity to waste daylight. He was hyperactive, like a tightly wound coil, just waiting for the right time to spring into action.

"Sure. I'm in," replied Kurt.

"We can play two on two if nobody's there," said Jeff.

Kurt didn't really like Jeff all that much, although he was part of their group. He thought Jeff was just too pushy at times, forcing him and the others into situations he created that they'd rather not be in. But nonetheless, he accepted Jeff for who he was.

They finally made it to the courts, thirty minutes later, after waiting on their friend Elliot Spencer.

Elliot was the blonde, non-athletic boy in their group, who was usually the one responsible for hold ups whenever they played together.

He was nerdy and whiney, a real klutz, but had been good friends with Kurt since kindergarten. Kurt had stuck up for him on multiple occasions, as bullies were apt to pick on him. Bullies were like water to Elliot, constantly changing and never ending.

They played a couple games on the court, before sitting on the benches, taking a little break to gain some much-needed energy. Kurt felt exhausted, plopping his butt down on the bench next to Jimmy. He was trying to conserve as much energy as possible, his bones still aching from the day before. They were about to start their trek back, when Ham and his goons showed up.

Ham, aka Jason Hildritch, was the unspoken leader of their neighborhood. If you didn't do what he said, he'd make a vow to ruin your day until you did. And with his goon squad always backing him up, it was his way or else.

Jimmy was friends with Ham, since their parents often hung out together, which made Kurt less of a target when it came down to it.

"What's up, Jimmy? What you doing with these losers?" said Ham, lightly laughing and pointing.

"Nothing Ham. Just finished up a couple games and we're about to head back."

"You haven't heard the news yet?" said Ham.

"What are you talking about?" asked Jimmy.

"Oh man. You're going to shit your pants," Ham laughed.

"Whatever," said Jeff.

"Dude, I got this," said Jimmy, slapping Jeff in the arm.

"Sorry," Jeff mumbled.

"What's going on, Ham?" asked Jimmy, curiosity eating at him like a virus.

"I've been three times already today," snorted Ham. "It's sick, man. You have to see it."

Kurt had no idea what he was getting at, and he didn't want to stick around any longer to find out. Ham was known to pick on him every now and then, for shits and

A is for Aliens

giggles, and Kurt wasn't too hot on the idea.

"Jimmy, I've got to get going," he said, giving him the eye.

"Yeah, run along," chuckled Ham. "You're too scared anyways."

"Scared of what?" asked Jimmy.

"There's a dead body in the alley behind the old warehouse over on Pike Street," said Ham, his eyes doing summersaults. "He's all fat and smelly from the sun, I think."

"What the..." exclaimed Elliot. "That's gross!"

"Waa waa, baby. I knew you guys couldn't handle it," laughed Ham, his belly jumping up and down.

"I'm not scared," said Kurt.

He didn't want to seem like a wuss around Ham, so he puffed his chest out and acted like one of the big boys. He did his best not to look intimidated, knowing that Ham could smell fear a mile away.

"Alright then chicken shit, let's go," said Ham.

He didn't really want to go, but he didn't want to be known throughout the neighborhood as a scaredy-cat either.

"You're scared," said Ham. "I sense it."

"No, I'm not," Kurt interjected.

"Come on, Jimmy. Forget these losers

and let's go," called Ham. Jimmy looked at Kurt.

"You coming?"

II

Kurt was in too deep now...too deep to back out. He was scared to see a dead body, but he couldn't stand the thought of Ham spreading rumors about him. He knew if he didn't go, he'd never live it down. As much as he hated the idea, he took a deep breath and slowly exhaled, releasing all his pent-up tension.

"You coming? Or are you too scared to see a dead body?" asked Ham, in a no-nonsense tone.

"Fine, I'll go," said Kurt.

Jimmy shot a look at him. "You know you don't have to...".

Kurt looked at Ham, then back at Jimmy. "Let's go," he said with stern eyes.

Pike Street wasn't too far of a walk, and being that they were young, they were used to the trek. As they hiked, Kurt did his best to remain silent and keep to himself. He listened carefully to what they were saying.

"You've got to see him, man," said Ham. "It's ugly."

"What happened to him?" asked Jimmy.

"Don't know," said Ham. "His throat is cut, and he has little red marks all over him, like he was stabbed or something. It looks like someone took a bite out of him, too."

"Ew, gross," said Kurt.

"Don't be such a pussy," laughed Ham.

"How did you find him?" asked Jimmy.

"I was walking through the alley, looking for stuff to bust up," said Ham. "And that's when I saw him lying there. He wasn't moving."

"Did you call the police?" asked Kurt.

"No way, man. Why would I do that?" Ham replied. "They'd probably think I did it or something. They'd throw me in jail for sure."

"I've never seen a dead body before," said Kurt.

"Me neither," replied Jimmy. "I bet he stinks."

"Yeah, he sure does," laughed Ham. "Smells like old feet and dead rats."

Ham was twice the size of the other kids, and he was very aware of the fact. He liked to throw his weight around whenever he could, using it to his advantage, forcing others to do as he said or suffer the consequences. He was a chubby kid, with curly orange hair and a constellation of freckles marking the right side of his face next to his ear. He was peculiar looking and had been given the nickname Ham, due to the fact that he sort of resembled a pig.

Kurt always thought Ham was weird looking, but he knew better than to let on about it. He stayed in his own head, thinking and listening as they carried on.

Kurt thought back to when he was younger, when tragedy had unfortunately and unexpectedly struck his family. He remembered walking home from school one day and seeing police cars lining his street. Up and down, from one side to the other. His heart had dropped at the sight, as red and blue lights danced on nearby walls and doors like morbid Christmas decorations.

He'd approached his front door and was startled to see two police officers standing there. They stopped him before he could enter, asking him if he lived there.

"Is this your house?" asked one of the officers. "Do you know who lives here?"

"I do. It's my house," said Kurt, nervously.

"Did you just get home from school, kid?" asked the officer. "Isn't it a little late to be getting home at this hour?"

"I had to stay after class with my teacher," said Kurt, his eyes shooting toward the dirt, doing his best to avoid looking at them.

"Where are your parents?" asked the officer.

"My mom's at work," he said, suddenly scared by everything that was happening around him. "She gets home at five."

"Well, what about your father?" asked the officer.

Kurt raised his head, "What's going on?"

"I'm sorry son, but you need to stay with us until your mother gets home," said the officer.

His mother had never fully explained to him what had happened that night, but he knew that whatever it was, it was really bad.

From what he was told, his grandfather, who'd been living with them since his grandma had passed away six months prior, had committed suicide that day, not long before he arrived home.

He never figured out the details of that day but made it a point to never forget the events that took place. The only thing he knew was that there was a lot of blood left behind. It had soaked into the carpet where his grandfather's chair used to sit, serving as an ominous reminder of the tragedy.

He never forgot the emotions that swept

over him in that moment, feeling like he was being strangled by some unseen force. He was frightened at the thought of what might happen in the future. Seeing death at such a young age was an engrossing experience. Something that he'd done his best to stay away from ever since.

He remembered watching his mother when she pulled up in the driveway. How she screamed at the sky, crying for her daddy. She'd snatched him up, grabbing him tight, hugging him like he'd float away without an anchor if the wind hit. It pained him to witness her in such a state of shock and confusion, as she broke down and just about fell to the floor.

Everything raced through his mind at once, as he walked quietly behind the other boys.

His mother had cried every night for weeks after her father's gruesome suicide, never recovering from the event. She often shut out those around her, who were simply trying to comfort her. She was a complete wreck, and as much as her loved ones tried, their attempts were in vain.

Kurt empathized with his mother and was extremely saddened by her apparent morose state. Nothing he said or did could snap her out of her grieving. Over the past few years her conditions had worsened,

A is for Aliens

and her livelihood was deteriorating at a rapid pace. Luckily for him, it was the first and only death he'd been subjected to.

However, the death was actually a blessing in disguise, being as his grandfather was a hateful, despicable old man. On occasion, he'd witnessed his grandfather physically putting hands on his mother and it bothered him. But as much as he wanted to intervene, he was too small to do anything except get hurt.

So, when he got home late from school that day, he was relieved to learn that he wouldn't have to deal with the stress of his grandfather any longer. The pressure had finally been alleviated, to an extent. Now he had to worry about his mother, who was uncontrollably spiraling downward into a deep dark hole.

But that was all in the past now, and Kurt was thankful it was. His mother was still in an altered state, but not nearly as bad as she had once been.

They turned down an old deserted road which was lined on either side with dilapidated, moldy, weather-beaten houses. Here and there windows were broken, some even boarded up to keep out vandals and the homeless population. The outside walls of every house were spray-painted with graffiti.

Suddenly, Kurt heard barking and looked up, prying himself from his thoughts.

There was a dog; a huge, intimidating dog, about ten feet in front of them, the whites of its fangs showing. It snarled at the boys, salivating through a set of sharp, clenched teeth.

Kurt looked at Jimmy, in a panic, and Jimmy looked up at Ham.

Ham glanced to his left, then bent over and fished an iron rod out of a pile of garbage next to him.

He wasn't easily intimidated and took a few steps toward the mutt. He was swinging the iron rod back and forth, in order to keep it at bay. Each time the dog lunged forward, Ham swung the rod with authority, letting the dog know who was boss.

Kurt thought about running and glanced back over his shoulder. Immediately Jimmy yelled at him.

"Don't even think about it. If you run, he's going to chase you."

"No doubt about it, said Ham. "Just stay still and don't move."

As slowly as he could, Jimmy snatched up a dirt clod and whizzed it at the mangy thing, hoping to scare it.

"No, don't," said Kurt, right as the dirt

A is for Aliens

clod left Jimmy's hand.

It bounced off the dog's side and hit the ground. The dog became agitated and snapped left and right as Ham attempted to hit it with his iron rod. He swung but missed the dog by a mile. It was like a high noon showdown, neither side backing down.

Kurt started yelling at the dog. "Get out of here! Go, you stupid mutt! Get!"

Back and forth they went, when out of the blue a wooden gate from one of the houses flung open and a middle-aged homeless woman stepped out. "What are you doing? Get out of here! You shouldn't be playing here. This isn't a place for children," she said as she slammed the gate closed.

The sound of the gate opening and shutting spooked the dog and it sped off with its tail tucked between its legs.

"Man, that was a close call," said Jimmy, scratching the side of his head.

"It wasn't gonna do anything," said Ham, chuckling.

"Maybe we should leave," said Kurt.

"Don't be such a pussy," laughed Ham, smacking Jimmy on the shoulder.

"Don't wuss out on me now," said Jimmy. "We haven't even seen the body yet."

III

As they were approaching the corner of Pike Street, they could see a man lying on the ground not too far ahead. He was behind an old automotive warehouse that hadn't been functional for the last decade or so. At one point in time it was a thriving business, but now it was vacant and covered in an overgrowth of weeds. Over the years, it had become the local hangout for the town trouble.

The name of the old business painted on the wall was quickly fading, and the roof had begun to crumble and cave in. Sections of the building were in ruins, gathering their fair share of nicks and scrapes over the years. One area of the back wall had been badly charred and burnt, stemming from an unwarranted attack by a few locals.

The backside of the warehouse was a known hangout for ruffians and the like. It's where they went to avoid the law and have a drink or smoke the occasional doobie. The police had long since stopped patrolling the development, making it a haven for those who wanted to do some partying without being hassled by the reds and blues.

As they drew closer, a feeling of unease settled in the pit of Kurt's stomach. He was watching the dead body as he strode toward it with the others, when out of the blue it began to shake and move, causing him to pause. His heart was pounding in his chest like a drummer trying to keep pace. It appeared as if the man was still alive and moving, until a mangy jet-black cat darted out from the opposite end of the street.

There was a slight draft heading in their direction and the odor emanating from the body caught the wind and piggybacked right toward them. The stench was so strong, the boys were forced to stop mid-stride and collect themselves. It smelled like fresh toast mixed with rotten tang, and sundried baby shit.

At first whiff it smelled semi-sweet, but as the boys drew closer, it quickly became too much to bear.

"Eww, that smells horrible," said Jimmy, grasping at his nose.

"It smells like bubblegum," laughed Ham.

"Yeah, bubblegum mixed with shit," remarked Jimmy.

"That's gross," said Kurt, his cheeks puffing out as his face turned a mild shade of green.

A is for Aliens

A block away a car horn blared its displeasure at an unseen soldier of steel, as the driver laid heavily on the nerve piercing, high-pitched horn. The sound was a good distance away, yet it was close enough to elicit a squeal and a jump out of Kurt-though still not enough to make Ham flinch in the slightest.

Ham didn't get scared anymore. He'd made a solitary vow to never again be frightened, after a horrifying encounter with his father and a belt, when he was younger. Ever since that night, instead of cowering and wishing he'd been cast in a starring role involving another family, Ham decided then and there to never again let someone dictate his emotional fortitude.

From that moment on, Ham stubbornly dedicated himself to becoming the big threat on his block, and of his class. He chose to bully those unable to defend themselves, as his own weird, twisted way of showing tough love to the kids who reminded him of his past.

Without warning, another trumpeting sound caressed the wind, apparently voicing its own disdain of the situation at hand. It sounded like two animals growling at each other, ready and waiting for the referee to signal the bell and commence the fight.

"Don't be such a wuss," Ham said to Kurt, who was caught off-guard by the unknown assailant expressing road rage to its fullest.

Even on such a beautiful day like today, it was impossible not to expect the pungent taste of madness to sweep through like a fierce beast and land its weary head on your plate. Days like this were common, the town continuously bustling with anger, some days more so than others. It was as if the town was under the veil of evil, flexing its bountiful bust attempting to attract, in some form or another, anyone who was willing to risk their life for a peek at what lies beneath.

Nevertheless, Kurt was mesmerized at how sturdily Ham was built. He was like an impenetrable fortress, surrounded by an abyss-plagued moat, filled with angry souls from another realm that would easily pick the skin from your bones if you weren't quick enough to react.

Nothing could poke through his protected, internal façade. Not even a rocket propelled by the hand of god. Neither could the love of his mother; not after the incident with his father years back.

Despite being provoked to let down the

sixty foot high wall he'd built in the recesses of his mind, Ham stood unwaveringly tough, as if he'd looked directly into Medusa's eyes and had been cast in stone - which people would pay good money for, and even stand in long lines in order to gaze upon the perfectly displayed carving of teenage pubescence.

Often Kurt wished he could be like Ham, or any of the other boys his age, happy, unafraid, and full of life. Sadly, that wasn't how he was wired. No matter how hard he tried, he knew he'd never be able to feel the way he truly wanted. He'd always be labeled as an outcast, never fitting in no matter how determined he was or how much he pretended. It just wasn't in the cards.

"Are you just going to stand there, staring off into space?" asked Jimmy, poking Kurt in the ribs.

"Huh? Oh, uh, I was just thinking," said Kurt as he snapped back to reality, wiping the drool from his chin.

Ham was poking the body with the pipe he'd picked up earlier, trying to open the wound on the man's neck. Ham had a morbid curiosity and was deeply intrigued to see what things looked like under the man's skin.

"Stop that," said Kurt. "You shouldn't

do that! It's not respectful to mess with a dead body."

Kurt had picked up the idea one day, after watching Reverend Joseph Marks perform his Sunday mass on television. The Reverend's speech had stuck in his head ever since. The man stated that the shedding of a human vessel was imminent and should be approached with care and treated with the utmost respect during the discarding process. The vacating of the soul was inevitable, but that did not mean that the vessel should be cast aside like a child's toy.

Kurt didn't quite understand what that meant exactly, but respect seemed like the right thing.

"He's dead," laughed Ham. "What's he going to do?"

"Just because he's dead, doesn't mean you can do whatever you want," stated Kurt. "Show some respect for the man. How would you like it if someone messed with you when you were dead? I bet you wouldn't like it too much, would you?"

"Shut up! Get over it already," laughed Ham, snorting at the statement made by Kurt.

"Hey, guys. Take a look at this," said Jimmy, kneeling over the body, closely inspecting the gash.

The cut on the neck was so clean, it appeared to have been done with the precision of a surgeon. Ham pried open the loose skin, reminding him of splitting a hotdog bun at a cookout.

Something caught Jimmy's eye and he tilted his head, attempting to get a better view of whatever was inside. There were thousands of little bugs crawling inside the deep gorge of the man's over-puffed neck. Tiny white larvae, around five to ten millimeters in size, had apparently orchestrated a musical for the group of onlookers, as they swayed together in unison like a chorus line. It was an entire choir of thriving life, all condensed into one dead man's neck.

Kurt pondered the little insects, wondering what it would be like if he'd been a part of that family instead of his own. He wondered how the larvae must feel, trapped in their own morbid life. Eating, growing, and eventually cruising the same potholed path, day after day, until death.

It was a crazy thought, how similar he and the insects were to each other. How they seemed to follow the same principles and routes as their counterpart did. The unfortunate rat race of daily bidding and the tough, unyielding struggles of making it all cohesive and concise. He finally understood the bugs, and, in turn, he understood himself.

His stomach grumbled with a low howl, like the teeth of a garbage disposal waiting hungrily for discarded food to shred. It rumbled and bubbled like a volcano on the verge of eruption. He could taste the vomit in his gut and the sour, mildew speckled contents asking to be delivered. He could feel the accentuated displeasure as bits and pieces trudged their way up toward the exit.

Mashing it down like packed dirt, Kurt stood sturdy, begging and pleading with the universe to let the nausea pass. Calming himself to a state of near meditation, he was able to withstand the floaties swarming his vision.

Jimmy looked at Kurt. "Are you alright, man? You look sick."

"I haven't eaten for a while. My stomach isn't too happy about that."

"Hungry?" said Ham, curiosity rushing out of him like a flood. "How can you be hungry at a time like this? Around a dead body? That's disgusting."

"I'm...I'm sorry," stammered Kurt.

"Why don't you eat one of these," said Ham, pointing the iron rod at Kurt, maggots squirming on the end. "If you're so hungry, take a bite."

Ham laughed as he hung the pipe in the air, fidgeting it left and right, up and down.

"Stop!" demanded Kurt, full of sudden rage.

"You're such a wuss," said Ham, continuing to purposefully wave the pipe directly in front of Kurt's face.

"I'm not!" Kurt snapped.

"Dude, don't," said Jimmy, glaring at Ham. "Come on man, just leave him alone."

"What are you going to do about it?" asked Ham, evil intentions scrolling through his eyes like a slideshow.

"Just leave him be Ham," demanded Jimmy.

Ham happily flexed his power, unafraid of neither one of the boys. He was never shy of displaying his physical prowess and dominance over others.

"Whatever..." said Ham. "You're a couple of pussies. I'm leaving."

Ham trotted down the alleyway, heading home. Kurt watched until he disappeared before expelling the breath that he'd been holding in. He had held his tongue the whole time, not wanting to say anything for fear of potentially infuriating the bully even more. He was relieved that Ham was

A is for Aliens

finally gone. He'd sensed Ham wanted to pick a fight, but he wanted no part of it.

Kurt glanced at Jimmy, who was so absorbed and engrossed with the dead body that he hadn't even looked up when Ham wandered off. Jimmy was kneeling, scouring the hand of the dead man.

"That's weird," Jimmy said to himself, unaware of Kurt standing behind him. The index finger, middle finger, and thumb, along with a fraction of the dead man's right hand, had apparently been gnawed off. Rugged marks formed a parameter around the missing flesh, like a crowd packing in to see a concert.

Jimmy was doing his best investigative work, closely surveying the hand, looking over every prospective cut, oblivious of his surroundings. He was so intrigued by the fact that something, whatever it might have been, had taken a bite out of the man's hand.

"Dude, check this out! Looks like something was eating him," said Jimmy, his face turning a shade of pickle green. "What could have done that?"

Kurt said nothing as he stood silently behind his friend. He was trying his best to remain calm and in control, as his emotions began to run wild. He hated feeling the way he did, but it was ultimately inevitable, and he knew it. He was never fond of the emotional turmoil that followed something like this, but it came with the territory. It was something he just had to put up with and accept no matter how much he disliked it. It was as much a part of his life as breathing, yet the feelings irked him anyhow.

Jimmy was still kneeling over the body, fascinated with the spectacle. He'd never seen anything like it before. It was just like the bodies he'd seen in the movies and on television, only paler.

Suddenly Kurt coughed, startling Jimmy and jarring him back into reality. Jimmy shot a look over his shoulder, only to find Kurt licking his lips like he was about to devour a bowl of his favorite ice cream on a scorching hot day.

"Dude, what the fuck is wrong with you?" Jimmy snapped. "That's just gross!"

Kurt's tongue darted out between his lips, flapping from side to side. Jimmy noticed a blankness forming behind Kurt's eyes, as saliva shot out from his mouth and tongue, spewing all over the dirt.

"Kurt, are you alright man? You don't look so good." There was no response. The lights were on, but no one was home. Someone, or something, else was in control, pulling the strings - the grand ole

A is for Aliens

Oz himself behind the curtain.

"Quit that already. It's freaking me out!'" blurted Jimmy, his eyes wide with fright. Kurt stood there, motionless, like a plant rooted in the earth.

Jimmy rose to his feet as an eerie feeling convulsed through his body, causing the hair on his arms to stand to attention. Instantly he knew something wasn't right. Before he could even form a thought, he watched as Kurt's eyes flickered, changing from one color to the next. Buckets of saliva made its way down Kurt's narrow, snake-like tongue. Suddenly, Kurt's mouth shot open and a strange noise emanated from it like a loudspeaker.

It was like a multilayered album track. A low grumbling draped over white noise, which seemed to be playing like an out of tune radio station. It was the strangest thing he'd ever heard.

Kurt's left ear drooped, shifting and twisting into an unrecognizable jumble of flesh. Two solid pointed white structures began growing out of the sides of the boy's head, protruding from where his ears once sat. He snapped his head backward and the skin fell slickly down around the nape of his neck, like he was removing his hood of deception.

A is for Aliens

To Jimmy the things on the side of Kurt's head resembled horns - horns made of bone. They curved around the back of Kurt's malformed head, the tips pointing upward, directed towards the sky; as if to communicate with some strange, higher power from beyond the stars.

Kurt let out a howl that caused Jimmy to lightly relieve himself in his pants. Jimmy had no idea what was happening to his friend, and he was badly shaken. It looked as if the devil had come to life right in front of his eyes.

The next thing he knew, Kurt's right arm fell off and hit the ground right in front of him. From the elbow down, the whole thing just fell into the dirt. Jimmy watched as a long slender tentacle sprung out in its place, replacing the detached appendage. The piece which had fallen off was now melting into a what looked like a puddle of plastic. A smile formed on the face of the thing, as it mocked and mimicked Jimmy's facial expressions. The boy watched as it changed shape to mirror his own appearance, before quickly changing to something else. He stood in awe as it cycled through what had to be hundreds of thousands of victims. And he wasn't one hundred percent sure, but he could have sworn that he saw Kurt's grandfather pass by as the thing continued changing shape.

Jimmy saw men, women, and teenagers appear and vanish as fast he could snap his fingers. But that wasn't the worst of it - not even close. What he saw that day would haunt him for as long as he lived, which might not be for much longer, from the looks of it.

Just before the thing slowed to a stop and rested on its true form, Jimmy witnessed it cycle from newborn to newborn, until what seemed like an entire ward of infants had passed by in a matter of seconds. He couldn't quite understand it, much less did he have time to think about what had befell his friend and all those people, including the poor, poor babies.

Suddenly the clouds growled and grit their teeth. Darkness strolled in, threatening the sky like some unseen army seeking death and destruction to all who dare to touch it.

Jimmy tried to plead with the thing, "Kurt, man, are you in there? It's me, Jimmy. Please don't hurt me, man! You're my friend! Please, please!"

The thing lunged at him and Jimmy ducked, keeping his life intact - for the time being. He knew he had to do something quick, but he couldn't think of anything. He decided if he didn't make a move soon, everything would cease to exist. His whole life was in jeopardy, flashing before his eyes. Everything depended on what he did at this moment in time, but before he had a chance to make an escape, a loud screeching sound drowned out everything and all he could hear was a horrific, ear-piercing screech like someone was clawing and scraping at the inside of skull. He fell to his knees in front of Kurt, desperately grasping at his ears, trying his best not to tear them straight off. He knew his life was over, and he looked up once more, shading his eyes as the wind picked up and a bright neon light pulsed directly overhead.

The sky was completely black, then instantly flooded with light. Over and over again it flickered, as all the trash and debris in the alleyway began to circle around them. Kurt, or what was at one time Jimmy's good friend Kurt, snarled and smirked proudly, viciously displaying a mouth of razor-sharp fangs, resembling rows upon rows of barbed wire. This couldn't be his old friend Kurt. They grew up living on the same street with and had known each other nearly their entire lives. They stayed the night at each other's

A is for Aliens

houses and rode bikes together. They played together and were always in the same classes all throughout school. They talked about girls and things that they dared not share with anyone else for fear of humiliation and torment for years to come. Yet there they were, and this was it; this was how it was all going to eventually end. The two of them, in some weird nightmare battling for survival and wondering who would come out on top, wondering who the winner would be.

Jimmy's heart sank in his chest. Everything was silent, so silent in fact that he couldn't even hear his own heart beating. He questioned whether he was actually deaf. Had he lost all his hearing or was this simply a dream and everything would be over in a matter of seconds? Was he going to suddenly wake up and realize that this was all just some wicked nightmare he'd made up in his own mind, or was it really some sick and cruel twist of fate?

He could see the thing gear up to come at him one more time, and he was ready to do what was needed. The wind picked up and trash pelted his back and sides. It felt like being sprayed with fresh tar on a hot summer day. It burned and hurt way worse than any pain he'd ever known in his short existence on Earth. Each time the light flicked on, he could see the thing inching closer and closer and he would look away right as the light cut out. In one of the flashes he saw cockroaches, larvae, and various other insects being swept up into the whirlwind and whipped around like they were fruit in a blender. He was about to lose his lunch when he was hit with something as tough as concrete and he blacked out.

IV

One year later...

He stepped out into the morning, as the sunlight hit him dead in the eye. Everything was vibrant and he was happy that it was his favorite time of the year again, the first day of the traditional summer break. He stretched and raised his arms above his head as he yawned, taking in the beautiful fresh morning air. He thanked the lord above that he was alive on this glorious day. Without warning, something hit him in the stomach and he nearly fell over. It felt like he had been punched in his midsection and he almost buckled with the pain.

The boys heckled and roared with

A is for Aliens

laughter. "You should have been paying attention," belted Jeff.

He stood up, gathered himself and grabbed the basketball. "Screw you guys," he said, and they all started laughing like a cackle of wild hyenas.

"Remember what happened to me this time last year, I'm just lucky to be alive," he said with a smile.

"Yeah, that's a day we will never forget. Rest in peace, dear friend," said Elliot as he made the sign of the cross on his chest. "In the name of the Father, Son, and the Holy Spirit. Amen."

They made their way down to the courts to play a few games of hoops, starting out the day as they normally did. After everyone had worn themselves out and were about to head home for some snacks and recuperate, one of the local boys who had been hanging out at the park approached the group.

"Hey, have you guys heard about it yet?" asked the boy.

"Heard about what?" said Jeff, glancing around at the boy and his friends.

The boy leaned in as if he was telling a secret that could get him killed just for thinking about it. He whispered, "Do you guys want to see a dead body?" and he chuckled.

A is for Aliens

Jeff turned and looked at his friend, "What do you say Kurt? Do you want to see a dead body?"

Kurt rolled his eyes, "Yeah, right."

The Blue World

Jeremy Megargee

We have come across countless light years, and I am weary now. The colonization ship is a rickety ruin that threatens to spill us out into the great black vacuum of space if we do not find a place soon. It creaks and groans like an elder well past the larval stage. The pressure is unfathomable, and I wonder what happens to us if the ship just falls apart. Perhaps shards of the hull will drift down to some paradise world that we overlooked. Maybe our lifeless biological matter will wash up on some lonely shore, and whatever lives on that shore will stare down at our remnants and open themselves to wonder.

I wonder often. It seems wondering is one of the few things that sustains me on this journey. It has been so painfully quiet, and even the seer-mothers in their skin sacks do not speak prophecies anymore. We have been too long in the void. The star shine is unkind up here, and what little light there is appears distant and cold. Is there only more nothingness to hope for? I kneel in the nights—nights everlasting—and I focus on the singular hope of something more. My sensory tendrils throb, my gills tremble, and an absence grows in my four-chambered heart.

I miss Bayoon. I miss home. We poisoned home. We infected it and soiled it with inaction. All of us became complacent in the face of devastation, and we realized far too late that a world isn't promised. It's a delicate thing, and even a world will crumble if slow and systematic damage is done to it over a lengthy period of time. Such was the case with Bayoon. It was never the goal of my kind to kill our world, but we did it all the same. We could not even mourn her before the shuttles began to launch. It was pandemonium. Stay and meet the final cocoon or flee and chase an uncertain future. I chose to flee. I chose hope beyond Bayoon—the only world I've ever known.

My salvation is this vessel, but it is also my prison, and if things don't change, it has the potential to become my tomb on the path to the final cocoon. A massive legion of us escaped before the end, and when this voyage began, the ship was bustling with us. The community hive thrived, and it was almost like being on the surface of Bayoon.

We are less than a thousand now. This endless travel has made sickly wretches of our once hardy kind, and the few left with working gills are so weakened that we rarely leave our individual hibernation chambers. There's nothing natural about the ship. It's just a hollow sarcophagus carting the few survivors of a dying race across empty star systems. We sense that on some level, and it burdens us even more. Never again will I swim in the lake-swamps of Syr. I'll not play another game of riddles with my brood-kin on the Islands of Som. I have forgotten what it used to look like when the suns would darken across the reeds. Even the scents of Bayoon are becoming lost to me, and it is anguish to let such memories fade.

I find that the name given onto me at the time of my hatching is hard to recall. Icarik, I am called, but the sound means little when chattered from the mandibles of my few remaining companions. Most of us pass each other in dull hazes, and each corridor of the ship has taken on the look of a bog worm decaying from the inside out. We are all frail now, and the threat of starvation looms. Our rations included enough nutrient discs to last literally lifetimes, but there have been moments of greed, sabotage, and disaster since this voyage began. What is left will not feed all of us for much longer. There were some that took to the bowels of the ship and turned cannibal, devouring their own and making a paste of kindred travelers. They smeared themselves in the bioluminescent plasma drawn from the veins of the withered and wounded, and it became clear that they'd gone brainsick amongst all these alien stars.

That wing of the ship was sealed and amputated from the hive, and the maddened eaters of their own floated off into the unknown reaches of a galaxy now far behind us. I doubt it's possible, but sometimes I still hear them shrieking from a part of the ship that doesn't exist any longer. Their broken verse became an inverted mantra in the end, and those of us with intact thoughts came to loath the implicated message.

A is for Aliens

"No worlds, no worlds, no worlds..."

It cannot be true. There *must* be another world out here somewhere. Something inhabitable. Something to take in the pitiful refugees that we have become. A place not of jagged rock and brutal storms, but of waters vast and islands aplenty. There is another Bayoon somewhere in this endless universe, and if we do not find it, our entire species expires, and what will there be left to prove that we ever existed in the first place?

We all take turns indulging in the long rest, but the long rest saps the sense of self and leaves us muddled upon each new awakening. I toss and turn in my own liquid vat while light years roll past, and each time I struggle up to the surface more of the precious water is lost, and more time has been sacrificed with no results. The vats are a poor substitute for the real thing. It is claustrophobic to languish in that wet dark, and it feels nothing like slumbering in the warm and bright ponds of Bayoon.

We have lost so much, and on some level, I don't think we even comprehend the weight of that.

A is for Aliens

The lethargia epidemic came shortly after the cannibalistic uprising. It's a mysterious disease that affects our kind during extended deep space travel, and it ravages us from the inside out. First the carapace turns soft and peels, and then the pain blooms in the thorax. It's a blistering horror, and we expire into curled up husks. Our patient zero was quarantined in the medical bay, but his corrupt organics had already smeared into numerous other denizens of the ship. The dead were placed into tube cylinders and ejected out into space, but by the time the disease had run its course, almost all my brood-kin had passed into the final cocoon. The phase to end all phases. Our death knell in the form of a silken box to hide the shame and the rot. There is nothing to do but mourn in the face of the final cocoon.

The hive trembles now, and the few of us left to protect the broodline are despondent to the point of catatonia. Only two pilots have survived. Four of them fell to lethargia, and a fifth was pulled down into the gloomy underbelly of the ship and made into a meal by the voracious rebels. The pilots that remain can usually be found staring with deadened eyes from a globular cockpit into the great absence that is space. Their limbs move, their mandibles click, and, if you were to lean down, you'd hear the little knocks of their four-chambered hearts, but aside from that there appears to be almost no life in their bodies. They have taken on the pallor of the fungal fallen, and on Bayoon such poor wretches would be planted into the coral and left alone, but up here that is not an option. They remain glued to their posts because otherwise we'd be drifting blind, and if anything would serve to carve out that last glimmer of hope, a ship without navigators would do it.

There is but one elder left on the ship. Her leadership is invaluable, and it's through her seer sight that we guide ourselves through the star corridors. We have come across a few planets with potential, but upon closer inspection, almost all of them have disappointed. Their atmospheres are too tumultuous, their waters too poisonous, or their terrain as barren as the lost desert of Crom. We have found nothing sentient in our travels. One little white planet caught our interest, but the scout we sent returned to tell us

A is for Aliens

that nothing remained down there but a miniscule planetary core and a surface crust covered in enormous weathered bones. Some massive species long since dead, perhaps for millions of light years.

The situation has looked dire, but now a new galaxy has unfurled in the flickering glow of the ship's dying lights. There are several planets in this solar system, and a great blistering globe of orange in the distance. The first of the planets was a little frozen speck not even fit for a frost whale. The others appear as enormous gaseous orbs, but the toxicity of such places prevents landfall. We draw closer to the prevailing star that burns in this system, and a rocky red ruin of a planet seemed promising, but upon closer inspection it's too stripped and desolate to support our race. Once again hope started to dissipate, and then we saw it.

The globe of blue and green. That perfect spinning promise. A world that sent our faulty sensors into overdrive, bleating out indications of water, atmosphere, terra, and even sentient beings. The news passed through our ranks like a flood, and mandibles click with excitement at the possibilities. This is what we've been seeking for what feels like eons. This is hope. This is life.

This is a world that welcomes, and it spells the survival of our species after the doom of Bayoon.

***

We have been orbiting the Blue World for quite some time. We are attempting to take the measure of it with failing equipment and outdated sensory devices. So far, we have gleaned little. Our communication carriers have not returned, and bellow greetings from the ship have gone unanswered. Our long-range mapping sensor reports an almost inexhaustible amount of suitable water, an abundance so profound that it makes the pools of Bayoon pale in comparison. We are having trouble pinpointing the nature of the sentient beings below, though. One estimation probe dictated that the living creatures down there number in the billions, but we have all agreed that the probe is malfunctioning. That number is astronomical and ludicrous. It is more likely that the probe copied a few lifeforms multiple times and presented incorrect data. The elder has attempted to use seer sight to understand the nature of the Blue World occupants, but her vision is blocked. She sees only flashing imagery and hears only incomprehensible sounds. Due to the communication silence of the Blue World, it is being assumed that the sentient race down there is akin to what we call a "rufkor" species. These are like the animals of Bayoon, beings that live and breathe but are otherwise limited in their capacity to form thought and exchange phrases. Our remaining biological brood-bringers believe that the species are inferior and likely not as advanced as our own. Long ago we developed weapons known as reed renders from a carved reed inlaid with a repelling brown juice that we form in our digestive system, and a projectile blast of this repellent liquid is enough to harm and dissuade any rufkor creature on Bayoon from attacking us. As a result, we conquered Bayoon and came to sit at the top of the evolutionary ladder. If we descend and encounter resistance, we'll do what we must with the reed renders to drive the Blue World's occupants into surrender.

A is for Aliens

It is savagery, but it is also survival. We have everything to gain and everything to lose here. We intend to dock on the Blue World surface even if it's the last thing our kind does.

***

Our resources have become almost nonexistent. Our rations are either spoiled or gone, and the pressure of deep space travel has beaten the ship into threaded parts, and if we stay up here much longer, the hive chambers will snap free from each other and we'll be sent spilling out into oblivion. We have only one chance. The elder voiced it while all the rest of us thought it.

"We must invade."

And that is what it will be. If the Blue World had no lifeforms then this would be nothing more than an exploration mission, but because of the circumstances, this will be an invasion. We are refugees, and we do not wish to harm, but if this colonization is not successful, our lives are forfeit. The ship lowers into the foreign atmosphere, and how the old rickety monster laments as it is battered and bruised even more. But the ship's suffering will soon end, because the Blue World is drawing closer, the white wispy blankets of moisture fading as we hover toward our fate.

We descend.

And soon after, we despair.

***

I, Icarik of Syr, have but a moment to marvel at the majestic beauty of the Blue World before chaos eats through my senses. Winged vessels of astonishing speed jet back and forth overtop us, cylindrical devices honed in on our ship, the vessels almost escorting us downward. These vessels are flanked with a legion of bubble-shaped mechanisms that float on whirring blades, and strange goggled faces stare out at us with alien indifference. We were not expecting this. We have never encountered...machines of this complexity before. Our own ship is just an organic drift hive grown in the bogs of Wyst, but these hovering monstrosities are all hard edges, blackened apertures, and sounds that threaten to puncture our hearing holes. They howl for us, and we are made small with the noise of those howls.

The ship continues to descend, and finally we settle with a gentle click into a vast field of greenery. There is a mammoth structure of White in the distance, and a pointed monument behind us that seems to stretch up and reach to the heavens. There is a metallic surface with an alien language inscribed upon it, some unfathomable message that reads "Washington, D.C.".

The mouth of the hull opens with a languished sigh, and all the heart-engines of the hive ship die at once. It will never rise again. The Blue World will act as its grave chasm, and what a shame for it to enter the final cocoon in such unfamiliar territories.

We file out with our tattered band of survivors, most of us injured and shambling, staring with obvious awe at the sights laid out before us. We clutch to our reed renders like useless staffs, and we chitter at each other for comfort. Our invasion has begun, but the inhabitants of the Blue World were prepared for it.

Our sensors weren't faulty. They were right. There are...billions of them. This field of green is populated with a huge contingent of their kind. They are pinkish giants covered in scraps of cloth, and in their hands they carry long metallic instruments with dark barrel bores, and all of these bores are staring at us. A much smaller creature darts out in front of our ranks, and a nervous brood-trooper brings his reed render down and hits it with a projectile of repellent juice. It resembles the rodents on our own homeworld, the only difference being a bushy tail. The juice hits the creature, but instead of dissolving it, the little rodent just shakes it off and carries off a nut in the opposite direction. We are aghast at this revelation. Our weapons don't even harm the lowest lifeform here, so how will they defend us against the towering kings of the Blue World?

One of them snorts out some sound, more incomprehensible language to our hearing holes. "Look at that. Heh. They spit like fuckin' grasshoppers..."

We are afraid now. We were wrong. We were so...terribly wrong. Our elder steps forward in a last-ditch attempt to communicate with the pinkish lords of this advanced planet. The rows of giants step aside, and their own leader comes

A is for Aliens

forward. This one is more ominous than the rest. He is bedecked in a dark cloth with a serpentine blue drapery around his neck. His skin is a sallow orange, and his hair is a wild nest—a nest fit for the crane crocs of Som. His eyes burn, and although there is hate on Bayoon, we did not expect to find it here.

It is here. It is in this one. He leans down to stare at the elder, and she withers under his gaze. A shining decoration is affixed to his cloth suit, some emblem reading "Make America Great Again."

The elder chitters out entreaties, and the Blue World leader merely cocks his head to the side.

"We are dying. We have come far. We have nowhere left to go. Bayoon is gone. We beg you. This Blue World is big enough for all of us."

A sharp smile etches across that orange flesh, and a curled fist rises. All the metallic instruments held in the hands of the other Blue World soldiers rise with it.

He speaks, and the poison in him drips on us.

"We are humans. We are great."

He leans closer to the elder, and his smile is gone.

"Fire & Fury."

The metallic instruments make dreadful cracking sounds, and little balls of destruction rain down into my kind. Thoraxes are pierced, wings are shredded, and our cold plasma splashes out to stain the terra of an equally cold world. We fall. We die. We meet the final cocoon.

So many light years. So much struggle and suffering. We thought it was at an end. We were partly right. We are at an end. It becomes clear far too late...

We came to the wrong world.

The Blagham Lake Ceremonies

Tim Jeffreys

Our lake has drawn people for years, but those folks who started coming here recently were different.

I can remember seeing divers on the lake when I was a boy and asking Dad what it was they were looking for. "Oh," he said. "Years ago, before you were born, something went down in Blagham Lake."

"Went down?" I asked him. "What do you mean, went down?"

"Something." I can remember the thoughtful look on his face. "It passed right over the road. I saw it. I was on my way to work. A yellow streak across the sky, something burning bright at the centre of it. Then…*boom!*"

"Boom?"

"I remember that day," Mum put in. "I'd just stared working at the library then. I'd arrived to start my shift when the whole place suddenly shook. We all thought it was an earthquake. They sent us home. I remember that. They said it wasn't safe."

"What was it? A meteorite?"

"There was something in the paper about it being this Russian space probe, Hep 3. Remember that, Mary?" Dad gestured at my mother, but she shrugged and shook her head. "It'd been out for years and years doing a tour of the whole universe, then somehow been pulled back to Earth. Crash landed right here in Blagham Lake."

"Is that true?" I said. I looked at Mum for confirmation, but she wore a doubtful expression.

"I don't remember that. I think it was a meteorite, like Johnny said. A small one, thank God. Not like the one that crashed in Russia a few years ago. Remember that? Windows blown in on all the buildings. Alarms going off all over the place. That must've been terrifying."

"No, no," Dad said. "It was in the paper. Hep 3, the Russian space probe. That's what those divers are looking for. They wanted a piece of it. A souvenir. Imagine holding something in your hand that has been further out in space than any man-made thing has any right to be. Right out past Jupiter and Saturn. There was talk of draining the lake a few years back so they could find it. All these scientists going out on the lake in boats with weird instruments like they were looking for the wreck of the Titanic. Don't you remember?" He went on before I could respond. "No, probably not. You were too little then. You wouldn't have noticed."

Used as I was to Dad's well-known embroidery of the facts, I wanted it to be true. I'd go out to Blagham Lake with my friends and we'd stand on the banks and look out over the grey-green surface of the water, imagining that it concealed something which had travelled into the furthest reaches of the solar system. The flat expanse of water, still but for wind-blown ripples, seemed to be taunting us. I pictured the probe sat intact on the lakebed, a capsule of wonders waiting to be opened up. Then at home in bed, I'd flick through astronomy books Mum got for me from the library, and I'd imagine the thing that was in our lake blasting past the gas giants; photographing the massive roiling surface of Jupiter, and storing away the secrets of Saturn's rings. Then onwards it had journeyed towards the mysterious blue worlds of Uranus and Neptune. I'd tell myself that all that knowledge, all that data, all those images of worlds unimaginably far away, gathered over decades, now lay submerged at the bottom of Blagham Lake; and I'd shiver with delight and with a strange cold terror at the thought of it. So close it was. So close. It was as if I could have dipped my hand in the icy water of the lake and touched something alien, something no human being should've had knowledge of.

It can't have been too long after that Dad had his accident. Mum died a few years ago. Cancer. I nursed her through the worst of it. She didn't want to die in some hospital bed; she'd always said that. I missed the fact that my friends were moving out and moving on. Going to university and getting married. Whilst I stayed at home. I got an office job with the local council. Too late to think about moving away now there's grey in my hair.

There's some comfort in the fact that I've remained in Blagham. Walking the familiar streets. Knowing the names of almost everyone I encounter. And, of course, there's still the mystery to occupy myself with, the mystery of what it was that went down in the lake more than four decades ago. There's stuff online that seems to corroborate my dad's theory that it was the missing Russian space probe, Hep 3. But I've also read that space probes rarely, if ever, return to Earth. These brave little craft (brave? I can't help imbuing them with human qualities!) usually ended up in orbit around other planets or crashed or expired on those planets' surfaces. What a lonely end!

I still walk the heath now and then, taking a path along the crest of the hill so I can look down on the lake. About three months ago, I saw a light in the water. I'm sure that's what it was, a light from deep down in the lake, rather than a reflection on the surface. There wasn't anything to reflect, the day being overcast. A dark day. No sun. There'd been that odd yellowish glow coming up from the murk at the bottom of the lake. I ran all the way home. I didn't tell anyone; I don't know why. Shortly afterwards I started to notice these odd types assembling on the banks of the lake. Men and women with greasy hair; or they'd be wearing dirty and ill-matched clothes. If you spoke to them and asked what they were doing, they'd stare at you and lick their lips, or grin and laugh. They were odd, pale people, with bulging eyes and fingers that looked to me too long. One day one of them, a man, followed me home and stood outside my front door until I thought about calling the police. All evening I couldn't settle, knowing he was there, wondering what he wanted. I had an awful migraine and had to lie down on my bed. When at last the tension in my skull eased and I was able to get up off the bed and look out the window there was no longer any sign of the man.

More and more of those odd people came. You'd see them in town sometimes, hanging around outside the supermarket. They'd camp out on the banks of the lake, build fires, and use rocks and stones to build pyramids and cairn-like structures. Some of those cairns were as tall as a man. Local residents started to complain. Those odd folks had become a nuisance, and whenever they ventured into town their strange behaviour frightened people. A journalist from the Yorkshire Post even picked up the story and ran an article under the headline: STRANGE CEREMONIES AT BLAGHAM LAKE.

I watched from the hilltop the day the police stormed in and broke up the camp. Those people didn't put up much of a fight; it was as if they didn't understand what was happening. Some of them ran to the edge of the lake and directed wild shrieks out over the water as if they were calling out to something, asking for help or giving a warning. Eighteen arrests were made that day. The next day the cairns were dismantled, and the tents torn down. A sign went up that read: NO LOITERING.

Twice more after this, I saw that yellowish light deep down in Blagham Lake whilst taking my evening stroll over the heath. I had a weird compulsion to go down to the water. The urge was so strong that I had to fight against it. I had the insane idea that if I started walking, I wouldn't stop at the water's edge. I'd keep going, wading out into the lake until my feet could no longer find purchase. It was after these two sightings that the headaches started; crippling migraines that didn't let up for days and forced me to take whole weeks off work. My doctor referred me to the hospital in Leeds, but nothing showed up on the MRI scan. As I emerged feet first from the tube inside the scanner, I amused myself with the idea that it was a little bit like being born. *A breech birth*, I thought to myself. *A breech birth of a full-grown man.* I then had a sudden vision of something egg-like floating in dark water. There was an eerie yellow glow, much like the one I'd seen coming up from deep in the water under Blagham Lake. The egg, or whatever it was, suddenly broke open and something long and sinuous emerged. It could have been a limb of some kind. There was something alive, jerking out from inside the egg. The vision made me catch my breath and sit half upright, so that I banged my forehead on the interior of the scanner.

The radiographer put a hand on my chest. "Easy, Mr Copeland," he said. "Take a deep breath. It's over."

The vision plagued my thoughts all day. I couldn't shake the feeling that I'd witnessed something being born in the murky waters of Blagham Lake. Something had been incubating down there for years, and now it had emerged. Was that it? I lay in bed tossing and turning at the thought of the thing I'd glimpsed in my vision, that thing – whatever it was – thrashing around in the shallows at the edge of the lake, eventually dragging itself up onto the bank, finding its feet and taking its first look around. I thought of Blagham, our little town, and all the people here with their small interests and narrow pursuits. And I thought of that thing whose birth I'd somehow been able to witness, staggering naked and shivering through the dark and silent streets, drawn by the lights in the sandstone houses where people slept with no knowledge of how their minds were soon to be undone forever with the arrival of this creature, this *whatever*, this new intelligence. All night, I barely slept. The vision I'd had as I emerged from the MRI scanner kept flashing back into my mind. The egg breaking open and the sinuous limb emerging. When I woke in the morning and drew back the curtains, the sun was risen, and sat on the crest of the distance hills, brilliant and blinding. A ball of torrid plasma was the only way I could think of it and it seemed terrible suddenly, broiling and destructive.

When I arrived at work my colleagues informed me that people had been gathering again at Blagham Lake. They'd apparently been there throughout the night. Townsfolk walking their dogs on the heath had reported what sounded like a rave taking place down there in the dark by the banks of the lake. Some said fires had been lit. Only, when the police had gone to investigate first thing that morning, the site was deserted. There'd been clear signs of activity, footprints in the mud and a couple of abandoned dinghies – yes, it looked like people had been out on the water – but not a single person remained for the police to arrest. One of the admin staff, Barbara – a woman in her early sixties and a fixture since long before I started in the job – seemed more concerned with me than this troubling development.

"Are you all right, John?" she kept asking me, her eyes holding my face. "Taking care of yourself, are you?"

"Yes, of course," I said, nodding. I was so tired and concerned with what I'd seen in my vision, and the news that those queer folk had returned to Blagham Lake, and of what it might mean, that I didn't fully register the look in her eyes, which I later recalled as a mix of shock and pity. Barbara pursed her lips, hesitating.

"It's just that you were always so smart," she said. "So well turned out."

"I'm fine," I told her, looking down at

myself, bewildered somewhat by her interest.

It was true that during this period I'd stopped worrying over my appearance and, yes, my personal hygiene had gone onto the back burner. However, I didn't realise the extent to which I'd let things slip until a few days later when I looked into the mirror and was shocked at the sight of my own pale and puffy reflection. I looked like I'd aged twenty years in just a few months. My eyes were bleary and bagged, my unwashed hair had grown long over my ears and my jaw had an uneven covering of greying beard. I had, too, been neglecting to eat regularly and the skin was drawn tight over my cheekbones, my clothes were baggy on me, and my fingers – when I held my hand up in front of my face — looked thin and elongated, somehow stretched.

Also, the house, the poor house, once my mother's pride and joy, had fallen into neglect. Immediately, I set to work, gathering up the unwashed plates and utensils I'd discarded about the various rooms, stuffing clothes into the washing machine, and bleaching down the work surfaces. Then I shaved and showered, wondering what had happened to me, how I'd let myself go to such an extent. It was true what Barbara had said, I'd always taken pride in my appearance, and I was embarrassed to think that I'd let other people see how frowzy I'd become long before I myself became aware of it.

***

It's been three weeks and those strange folks haven't returned to Blagham Lake. I walk the heath every morning and every evening, but there's never a light in the water now. Is that what I'm looking for? Is that why I go there? My migraines have gone too; at least for the time being. I'm feeling more myself these days. Now when I see Barbara at work she smiles, looks relieved, pats me on the shoulder and says something along the lines of: "There he is." As if the person I'd been during that brief period of slovenliness hadn't been me at all but someone else; a fake, a fraud, an imposter.

I think about how some of those people who gathered at the lake had gone to the water's edge when the police descended on them and shrieked at the water. I'd thought at the time those shrieks were cries for help or some kind of warning — to what I had no idea. But now I think I heard something different in those shrieks. They weren't pleas at all. They were reverential. Venerating, you might say. And the people making them were on their knees at the water's edge as if they were...

Worshipping?

Had they been performing some kind of strange ceremony after all, just as that article in the Post had suggested?

I know. I know. None of this makes sense.

There's one final thing to confuse the matter further. When I went for my usual walk over the heath this past Sunday, I decided to walk down to the lake. In the water lapping against the banks, something floated. I knew what it was immediately. It was a piece of panel, a piece of solar panel, of the type I'd seen in pictures of space probes in the books Mum used to get me from the library. Could it be a part of Hep 3? Could this be proof at last of what really crashed in Blagham Lake? My hand shook as I bent down to grab it from the water. I remembered Dad saying: *Imagine holding something in your hand that has been further out in space than any man-made thing has any right to be.* And I stopped reaching for that piece of panel and rose to my feet. I just couldn't bring myself to touch it. It was as if I thought all the things the probe had encountered out in deep space would be transferred to me the moment my fingers touched this small part of it. And whereas once, as a boy, this thought might've excited me, now it filled me with fear and foreboding. I turned my back and struck for home.

I knew though that I would look for that piece of panel again when I next returned to the lake. Perhaps later that day; perhaps the day after. I would not be able to rest until I saw it again. I would want confirmation that it was something man-made that had crashed into the lake, something returning home from a long journey out in space. Events of the last few months, and the thoughts and feelings these events have inspired in me, I hope to write off as my own wild imaginings.

Better then, I thought to myself as I strode back up the hill towards the heath, *to go and fetch the piece of panel now, to hold it and console myself with it. If I come back tomorrow it may be gone.*

But no, *no!* I kept on walking. And as of now, I haven't been back.

I keep an eye on the news, and the local papers. What I'm looking for, waiting for, I'm not entirely sure.

Berserk

Mawr Gorshin

"Mr. King, I have to be honest with you," Joe Stewart, one of Louis King's general managers, told him as they left the company building, KingCorp, and walked into the parking lot around 9:05 that night. "The workers are going to complain—and I mean noisily—when you announce the pay cuts tomorrow."

"So, let 'em complain," the boss said. "Let 'em make as much noise as they like. What are they gonna do, quit? In this economy? Are they gonna unionize and go on strike? I'll get a bunch of scabs to replace 'em so fast, their heads will spin. I'll..." He suddenly looked up at the night sky.

"What is it?" Joe asked, then he too looked up at the stars. At first, it seemed as though a group of stars were flying straight at the two men, but as the little lights came nearer, they hardly grew in size at all. They were *not* stars; they were tiny white circles.

Still, they got closer and closer to the

men, flying at hurtling speed.

The light they collectively shone got so bright, it was blinding. The men's eyes hurt; they put their hands in front of their faces.

"Wait!" Louis said. "They're gonna hit us! *Aaaah!*"

A huge bright light flashed over the two men as the tiny white dots struck. Joe seemed unaffected, but Louis fell to the pavement, swinging his arms and kicking his feet, as if trying to get some wild animal off him.

"Get them away!" he screamed. "Get them off of me!" But the lights were gone. Nothing seemed to be there.

"Sir, nothing's attacking you," Joe said, offering his hand to help his boss back up on his feet. Mr. King took his hand and got up, though he was still shaking and swatting with his free hand at enemies invisible to everyone except him. "Sir, you're *fine*," Joe said calmly. "No more lights. They're gone. There's nothing to be afraid of."

"They're still here!" King shouted, swatting with both hands now. "Little white dots of light, trying to get inside me. Why can't you see 'em?"

"'Cause they're *gone*. There was a flash of light, then nothing. I don't know what it was, but in any case, it's gone now. Don't worry about it. You should just accept it."

"*Accept* it? They're trying to take over my body!" His body was shaking as much as his voice was, his hands and feet swatting and kicking at little lights that only he saw.

"Trying to take over your body? Little white dots of light?"

"I see 'em all around me. Don't you?"

"No. Not at all," Joe said, sneering in disbelief at his boss.

"Why don't you see them? They're *everywhere*. Hovering. Waiting for me to let my guard down." King kept swatting, kicking, and shaking.

"Maybe I should take you to a hospital, Sir."

They got in Joe's car, but King wasn't able to stop the lights from getting in with them when he opened the front passenger's door. As Joe was driving, Louis kept swatting at the tiny balls of white light.

"Mr. King, your swatting is making it very difficult for me to drive."

"I can't help it, Stewart. *Ungh!* Just get me to a doctor as soon as you can. What are these things, aliens or something?"

What? Are you crazy or something? Joe wondered. "I don't know, sir." They arrived at the nearest hospital after ten minutes. Once seated in the waiting area, they were fortunate enough not to have to wait long, for there was only one patient ahead of them, already being taken care of. As they sat together, though, King kept on fidgeting, swatting, and kicking. Joe looked around with wide eyes and a reddening face.

"The doctor will see you now, sir," a nurse called out to Joe after only a few minutes. He and King went into the doctor's office.

"OK, what seems to be the problem?" the female doctor asked.

"Doctor, you may want to take Mr. King here to the psych ward," Joe said. "I'd say his problem is in his head. He seems convinced that small white dots of light are trying to attack him."

"It's *real!*" King shouted, still shaking and swatting. "They're trying to get inside me!"

"Mr. King, please have a seat and try to calm down," she said, gesturing to a chair that King then sat in.

"Doctor, I hate to rush off, but there are some things I need to take care of," Joe said.

"If you could just fill out a form or two for us, explaining what happened to Mr.

A is for Aliens

King as you understand it, that would be really helpful," she said.

"OK, as long as it doesn't take too long," Joe replied.

"It won't," the doctor told him, giving him a couple of forms and a pen. She then opened the door and got her nurse's attention. "Doris, could you come in here and hold Mr. King while I give him a sedative?"

"Yes, Doctor Culic," the nurse said. She entered the room as the doctor prepared the sedative, then she held King by the arms and struggled to keep him as still as possible. Joe was filling out the forms for King as the doctor approached King with the needle.

"Don't sedate me!" King shouted. "These things will get me!"

"What things, Mr. King?" the nurse asked, in a voice that shook from the struggle, feeling her grip on him loosening.

"The aliens!" he shouted, then broke free of her grip and ran from the room screaming.

"Call the orderlies!" the doctor told the nurse. Joe gave her the completed forms.

"Here you are, Doctor. Again, I'm sorry, but I really must be going now. I have a lot to do; as a manager of Mr. King's company, I have to deal with his employees, and it can't wait."

"That's OK, Mr... Stewart?" Dr Culic said.

"Yes," Joe replied.

"We'll take it from here. Thank you, and good night." Joe left the hospital and the orderlies arrived.

"Good, you're here," the doctor said. "A patient has gone berserk, running around the hospital and screaming. I need you to find him and bring him back to me so I can give him a sedative."

"Yes, Doctor," the two men said together, then left to search for King. Two minutes later, they had him in one of the halls. While they were restraining him, struggling to keep him still, the doctor approached him with the needle.

"Just take it easy, Mr. King," she said. "This is only a *mild* sedative; it will calm you down. No one's going to hurt you."

"Doctor, you don't understand!" King grunted as he fought, in all futility, to get free of the orderlies. "I need to be alert! If I'm doped up, the aliens will get inside me...control my body. *Ungh!*"

"Aliens?" one of the orderlies said with a sneer.

"There are no aliens, Mr. King," Dr Culic said, sticking the needle in his arm. "There. We'll get Doctor Reynor to talk to you, and you can tell him all about it." Within minutes, King, in his doped-up stupor, stopped shaking.

***

He was taken to the psych ward and was sat in Dr Reynor's office with an orderly standing by just outside as they waited for the psychiatrist to arrive. As King sat in a chair before Reynor's desk, he thought only of the small, glowing dots of light hovering all around his head, white dots that only he could see.

They were staring at him. He could feel it. They were all like tiny, white, judging eyeballs. Their watching felt as if it were burning into his skin. Waiting for their chance to strike...to get inside.

He sensed them communicating in his mind, and he knew they understood his thoughts.

We won't come inside you against your will, they told him. *But if you keep refusing us, things won't end well for you.*

Keep away from me! he said in his thoughts. As doped up as he was, he still had enough clarity of thought to make his wishes known to them. *Stay out of my head!*

The people in this hospital already

regard you as mad, they told him. *If you continue to resist, you really* will *go mad.*

You won't take control of me, King thought. *I won't let you.*

It's not about taking control, they said. *It's about you learning to accept the new reality.*

You taking away my entire world? he asked mentally. *Stealing my property? My money?*

He looked up at a picture of the psychiatrist on the wall. The eyes looked down into his. The mouth opened. It said, in a human voice only King could hear, the aliens' answer: "We're only giving back what you stole, and are planning to steal, from your employees."

King shook so much from his hallucination that it was as if the sedative was wearing off.

Is the sedative...making me...see and...hear things? he wondered.

A huge mouth opened on the side of the desk facing him...a large black oval opening and closing as the words came out.

"No, it isn't the sedative; it's your mind falling apart," it said in a hoarse, bass voice.

"Oh...shit," he grunted, blinking and flapping his eyes open and shut in the hope he'd see more clearly, and not see what couldn't have been.

The hovering dots of light were moving in circles around his head, some rows clockwise, others counter-clockwise. Some rows of lights moved closer to his head and face, others further away. These rows moved back and forth before him.

"Why...are you...doing this...to me?" he slurred. A laptop on the doctor's desk spun around to face King. It opened and closed like a flapping mouth, saying, "We aren't doing this to you. You're doing it to yourself."

"How...am I...doing it...to myself?" He slouched so much on his chair that he almost fell off.

"By not accepting us," a wastebasket by his right foot seemed to say by moving its top rim like a pair of lips.

King shook so much from the sight of this, that this time he *did* fall off his chair.

"Oof!" he grunted, hitting the floor on his right side. The daydreaming orderly, sitting in a chair just outside the office, didn't hear anything.

King now lay on the floor on his back. The tiny lights were floating over his head, several inches above his face, all lined up in perfectly straight rows and columns. They looked like a flat, rectangular screen.

Still, they felt like so many eyes staring at him...*waiting.*

The carpet under and around him was moving in ripples like the waves of the ocean. The waves would push him and make him roll over from left to right. Sometimes he'd bump into the tipped-over chair or hit his legs against the sharp wooden corners of the square legs of the desk.

"Unff!" he'd groan every time. Still, the absent-minded orderly would never notice any sound in the room. Finally, after a few hours, Dr Reynor—who, to the annoyance of the hospital staff, had made himself unavailable by leaving his phone turned off—arrived. The orderly stood up to address him.

"He's in your office, Doctor," he said. *Where the hell has he been?* he wondered. *The only shrink available in the psych ward, and he's always leaving his phone turned off.*

"Thank you," Reynor said in sighs of annoyance at having been dragged back in to work at night. "You can go." The orderly left, and Reynor went into his office.

King was still lying on his back on the floor. Only he saw the rippling, wave-like movements of the carpet, and only he heard the voices of the picture, desk, wastebasket, and laptop.

"Mr. King?" Reynor said, as he looked down at his dazed patient. "Would you like to sit on the chair?" He picked up the chair and reset it on its legs.

King remained lying supine on the carpet, acting as if the psychiatrist hadn't said anything.

"I guess you don't want to," Reynor said, before sitting on the chair himself. "Very well. What's troubling you?"

"You won't believe me," King said with a sigh, his eyes locked on that screen of white dots hovering over his face. "I'm not sure…if *I* believe myself…anymore."

"Your eyes seem to be focused on something. What do you see?"

"I see…rows and columns of small, white dots of light. They're all perfectly aligned, in straight rows and columns."

"I see. Why do you think they're there?"

"They want…to come inside me."

"Do they want to take control of your body?"

You must accept the new reality, the dots of light told King in his thoughts. He took his eyes away from Reynor to focus on them. *You'll tear yourself apart if you don't accept us.*

"Mr. King?" Reynor asked. "Are they talking to you?"

"Yes."

"What are they telling you?"

"That I must accept them," King slurred.

"That you must let them enter your body?"

"Yes." The sedative was beginning to wear off.

"If they go inside you, what do you think they'll do to you? Will they kill you?"

"I don't know. In a way, maybe." King looked over at the window on the wall to the left as one enters the office. The window opened and closed like a talking mouth.

We will right all the wrongs you've done to those beneath you, it 'said'. Reynor looked behind him and in the direction of the window.

"Are the lights over there?"

"No," King said. "They're floating over my head."

"Why did you look over at the window, then?"

"Because it was tal..." King avoided Reynor's eyes in embarrassment.

"Was the window...*talking* to you?"

"Oh, God," King said, a tear running down his cheek. "I'm losing my mind."

"Let's not worry about whether what you're seeing and hearing is real or not. Let's just try to get to the root of the problem. What did you hear the voice say?"

"It said, 'We will right...all the wrongs you've done...to those beneath you'."

"The little lights will right those wrongs?"

"Yes."

"Are they aliens?"

"Yes, I think so. They came from...the night sky. They looked...like stars at first."

"They told you that you've done wrong," Reynor said. "*Have* you done anything you feel guilty about?"

"No. What I've done...is not personal. It's strictly business."

"And what have you done?"

"I've decided...to cut the pay...of many...of my workers. I have no choice...I have...to cut costs."

"And that isn't making you feel at all guilty?"

"No. It's just business."

"Are you sure it isn't making you feel guilty?" the doctor asked again.

Of course he isn't sure of that, a tall plant, in the corner of the room opposite the window, seemed to say, a pair of large leaves flapping apart and together like a mouth.

"Shut up!" King shouted at the plant in slurred words.

"What did the lights say to you?" Reynor asked.

"Oh, they...doubt me as much as you do," King said.

"And *you*, Mr. King?" the psychiatrist asked. "Do *you* have any doubts about your belief that you're free of guilty feelings?"

"Oh, so you're judging me now? You're calling me an evil, greedy capitalist? Is that it?!" Raising his head clumsily, King slurred his words like an angry drunk.

"No, not at all. I'm not interested in the morals of your business practices. My concern is with your mental state. I'm merely trying to get at the root of what is upsetting you. I'm saying that you, in your unconscious mind, are judging yourself. You know that these pay cuts are going to hurt your employees, even if you can't help making them. You know there's going to be an angry reaction among your workers. The stress of all this is making you push the guilt outwards, to project it..."

Suddenly, Reynor noticed a red, jagged crack along the middle of King's face. Reynor's eyes and mouth widened; he froze in his chair.

"What the—?" he began. "What's happening to your—?"

"What?" King said, his face cracking more. He only dully sensed the pain, thanks to the slowly fading effects of the sedative.

The crack was spreading down his neck, his chest, all the way down to his crotch. One long, jagged red line, out of which smaller red cracks emerged at the sides, like tiny tributaries of a small but long, red river. From those 'tributaries' sprang other, even tinier cracks, until his entire body began to look almost like a red grid of larger and smaller cracks.

"Oh!..." he grunted.

"Oh, my God!" Reynor gasped, then got up. "I'll go get help. This is beyond anything I can do." He ran out of his office and King could hear him in the halls shouting, "I need some help over here! Dr Culic! Help!"

The main crack in the middle of King's body was widening. The jagged red line was thickening. Blood was pouring out from the cracks.

Yet he stayed alive.

"Ah!" he moaned, feeling the pain grow stronger and sharper now. Those dots of white light continued to float over his head in the shape of a flat screen.

We aren't doing this to you, Mr. King, they told him in his thoughts. *You're doing it to yourself. Never forget that.*

"Ah!" he groaned, then his voice was cut off sharply. His body broke in half, the two haves drifting apart and settling at the opposite walls of the office. A pool of blood painted almost the entire carpet a reddish-purple colour. Any onlooker there would have seen such exposed things as his brain hemispheres, his dissected heart and stomach, and his mutilated intestines.

Yet still, King wouldn't die. The dots of light were sustaining him.

His halves sat up against the walls, lifted by the power of the white dots that hovered over both of them. New mouths were formed out of the holes made from his split stomach halves; through these mouths, the two halves of Louis King communicated with each other.

"It's all your fault that this has happened to us," the half sitting under the window said in a grunting, almost porcine voice. "Your greed, your selfishness, and your insatiable appetite for money."

"You're no better, you self-righteous hypocrite!" oinked the other half, which sat next to the plant. "Don't you go projecting your guilt onto me!"

"I'm the part that doubted all the bad business practices, not you," the first half

A is for Aliens

said. "I'm the part with the guilty conscience. You never felt any remorse!"

"You enjoyed the benefits every bit as much as I did," the second half said. "Enough with your holier-than-thou attitude!" An orderly, having heard the last part of the conversation, poked his head in the room.

"Oh, my God!" he said. "One half is as...holey...as the other!"

Reynor and Dr Culic entered the office. The female doctor gasped.

"What the hell happened to him?"

"I was just talking to him about his delusions," Reynor said. "Then, inexplicably, his body began to tear in half, right before my eyes."

"As you can see, doctors," the stomach of the first half said, the dissected sack flapping open and shut like a mouth, its inner liquids having emptied out onto the floor with all the blood, "I wasn't suffering from delusions."

All three onlookers froze, their eyes and mouths all agape.

"It's talking...through its *stomach?*" she asked.

"The aliens can do amazing things, can't they?" the second half said from its flapping stomach-mouth.

"Aliens?" the orderly asked, sneering

and looking askance.

"The white dots of light?" Reynor asked.

"Yes," the second half said.

Now, where all the smaller cracks in the dissected halves were, those jagged red lines widened, and the pieces separated and fragmented. All the pieces hovered in the air. More blood dripped onto the carpet.

The eyes popped out of their sockets and fell on the floor, rolling on the carpet toward the three onlookers.

Dr Culic screamed when the eyes rolled together and met at her feet, the irises looking up at her.

All the floating, fragmented body parts fell to the floor in gory piles. Their colour dulled. King was finally dead.

The white dots of light appeared, about fifty of them hovering in the air at eye-level with the orderly and the two doctors. As they hovered, they swayed back and forth. Reynor, Culic, and the orderly could feel the lights staring at them as if they were disembodied eyeballs...sizing the three up...getting ready to strike.

"So, what do we do now?" the orderly asked.

You join us, the lights told them mentally, *or you die.*

"I see," Reynor said. All the lights flew

like fired bullets at the three. A blinding flash engulfed them.

The next morning, Joe Stewart arranged a staff meeting in the KingCorp building, at which everyone arrived by 9 AM.

"Thanks for coming," he told them. "You must be aware, judging by the frowns on your faces, of the rumours about budget cuts in the company."

"You'd be referring to our cuts in *pay*," an angry woman said among the crowd, who now echoed her anger in indistinct mumbling.

"The company can't help it if they have to cut costs," a young man among them said. "It's company policy, and it's our duty to stand by it."

"There he goes again," the woman said. "Bootlicker Brad."

"Shut up, Barbara!" he said. "Better a pay cut than no job at all, in this economy."

"There won't be any pay cuts," Joe said. "Nor will there be any firings. Have no fears about any of that."

"Why is that?" Barbara asked. "Did King grow a heart or something?"

"No," Joe said. "He died last night."

"He *died?*" she asked, almost smiling. Now, the indistinct mumbling among the workers was one of shock.

"What happened?" Brad asked. "How did he die?"

"The story is very strange," Joe said. "The people in the hospital can't explain it. Apparently, he went mad for no known reason, ran berserk around the hospital, and had to be subdued by the orderlies; later, after being sedated and talked to by a psychiatrist, his body—and this is the strange part—was torn to pieces...by some...unexplainable force. The staff couldn't understand it."

There was more indistinct mumbling, with a few titters mixed in.

"Look, don't laugh at the messenger," Joe went on. "I'm only repeating the weird story they told me. All that matters as far as you're concerned is that your jobs are safe, and your salaries won't be cut. I've discussed Louis' death with his son, Peter, who as you know was never on good speaking terms with his father, and he'll be taking over the company. Peter has always been more sympathetic to us than he ever was with Louis, as you know, so I can assure you that his promise not to cut your pay or to fire you is genuine. All is well on our end!"

Cheers were now heard among the workers. Only Brad, who was first called

'Bootlicker Brad' by Peter two years ago, didn't cheer for his new boss.

"And now," Joe said. "I have one last thing to do. Just relax, all of you, and look straight into my eyes."

"Why do we have to do that?" Brad asked.

"Just indulge me," Joe said. "You'll all understand why in a few seconds."

Everyone looked into his eyes. A huge flash of light shot from Joe's eyes and enveloped the crowd of workers; then it disappeared as quickly as it had appeared.

Everyone stood calmly, as if nothing unusual had happened, as if no explanation were needed...everyone, that is, except Brad.

He was lying on the floor, shaking, kicking, and swatting at something visible only to him.

"Brad, what's wrong?" Barbara asked coolly.

"Get it away from me!" he screamed. "Get it off me!"

"Brad, nothing's attacking you," she said, offering her hand to help Brad back on to his feet. Her face, like everyone else's apart from Brad's, remained stoic.

"Never mind him," Joe said. "Just leave him here. We have important things to do. If he doesn't accept the new reality, his destruction will be *his* doing, not ours. Let's go."

They all walked out of the room in single file, the last of them turning off the light and leaving Brad alone in the dark to scream and fidget on the floor.

All he saw was black…and small, glowing white dots.

A is for Aliens

The Prairie Lures

Mark Anthony Smith

I don't know if I can go through it again. Even in the cold light of day my palms are sweaty. It was supposed to be the trip of a lifetime. Gosh! I remember being told I was going to Canada. I was asleep in the wagon at the time. I nearly bloody fell out the door when the Staff Sergeant told me. I thought I'd get charged for kipping. But he just laughed as I lunged forwards and said, "Driver Phelps. Pack your kit. You're going to Canada for three months." My parents were thrilled, of course. Most of the other lads were off to fight in The Gulf.

I was serving in 'The Royal Corps of Transport.' Our job in Alberta was to support the Tanks on Exercise and drain the town of Medicine Hat of alcohol. We soon got used to cross country driving down the slippery Rattlesnake Road at British Army Training Unit Suffield or BATUS for short. I never got used to the sub-zero temperatures though. It was bitterly cold on the Prairie. You had to wrap up at night.

A is for Aliens

I went out to support some Infantry lads on Patrol. It started with a kick as I was woken up from a deep sleep. "It's your stag, mate." I swore. It was 2am and I had to get out of my sleeping bag to sit in a trench for two hours. I took a deep breath, counted to ten, and faced the biting winds. The lad was pleased to be relieved of his duty. I begrudgingly took his place as he muttered "thanks" and I grunted. My rifle was freezing cold and I had to wake up, as I leaned against the parapet, keeping an eye open for enemy patrols. I lit a cigarette and cupped it so the cherry wasn't visible to anyone that might have been doing a Reconnaissance. I really couldn't be arsed at this time of night.

There was a cluster of trees, to my right, and flat open ground elsewhere. I felt so pissed off and tired. It was cloudy. My night vision started to improve as I stubbed my cigarette out. Then, I noticed lights in the trees. I straightened up. They swam about like Will o' the Wisps. I was mesmerized. Then I looked at my watch. The two hours of guard duty had flown by. I was relieved at 4am.

I didn't think of the pleasant distraction in the trees for long as I shivered in my sleeping bag. I soon warmed up and sleep took over. I was later shaken again. The

A is for Aliens

usual rude awakening. I counted to ten and unzipped my bed to face the cold morning. I had a quick strip wash that nipped my testicles and shaved. Then I ate porridge from my mess tin.

The day was spent cross country driving and servicing the Tank Targets. I fed the gophers some brown biscuits and night fell. I was called upon to join a Reconnaissance Patrol. There were reports of enemy in the woods.

We set out to see how many there were and what sort of kit they had. We might have needed to call in the Artillery or an Air Strike if they had field guns. Our job was to stay out of trouble and not be seen. We just had to report our observations. Me and five other lads set out on Patrol. But only I came back. I can still see the fucking entrails...

There was no light as we entered the forest. We had to ghost walk through the trees as there were twigs underfoot and it was prime trip wire territory. The sky was cloudy again. We took our time so as not to alert anyone. The roosting birds in the trees were calling to each other. I found this unusually eerie. We were cautious. Then, a muffled scream. I dropped to the ground. There was confusion. I waited. "Someone has snatched the tail-end

A is for Aliens

Charlie." *Oh, for fuck's sake,* I thought. We had to find the last man in our patrol. But we didn't. We re-grouped. There were arguments and lads lashing out. "Let's go back!" "Let's carry on!" "Oh, for fuck's sake."

We decided to abort the Recce and return to base. The missing man would be at our last rendezvous, we thought. But he wasn't. And the trees were closing in. We quickened our pace as what little humour turned to fear. This wasn't a daft joke after all. There was something amiss. I thought there were shadows in the trees. We hurried. The shadows were real. And then I felt suddenly alone. I was cut off from the patrol.

I won't lie. I was absolutely shitting myself. What the hell were those lights last night? They'd been strangely calming. But now the forest was a living hell. I was lost and disorientated. I stopped to find my bearings. Then I saw the bastards. They must have been nearly ten feet tall. They weren't Sasquatches. But they walked like men. I will never forget those dark red eyes. It was like looking into a blood bath. I screamed, "Help!" Any notion of being tactical had passed. I was fighting to stay alive. I must have hit every single branch as I ran. I dropped my kit. Then I threw up. There were steaming innards hanging off a branch like perverse Christmas tinsel. It was a complete mockery. I threw up again. Then I ran. I ran all the way back and passed out.

On my return to Colchester, there were rumours. None of the lads had come back off the patrol. "You'll be seeing The Commanding Officer for manslaughter," some of the lads retorted. "Fuck off!" I snorted. I was confused. I needed peace and quiet. Whatever those things were, they weren't wolves or escaped animals from the zoo. I think they were something more, something not of this world. I mean, they were nearly ten foot tall.

I will never recover from my Canadian trip. It was supposed to be a once in a lifetime blessing. But I lost some good mates to those cannibalistic savages. I'm hoping to get a job on Civvy Street now. But until then, I try to stomach a few books on Indian Folklore. It's too much.

The Pioneer

P.J. Blakey-Novis

I always knew they were out there. I think that most of us did. It seemed pretty unlikely that we'd be alone in the universe, but it still felt like fantasy to actually make contact. I'd always held out some hope that, should we ever encounter a species from beyond the stars, they would be friendly. Surely, we would have a wealth of knowledge to learn from one another? Maybe we could even create a trade agreement with these other beings, something mutually beneficial. Perhaps I was too optimistic in those days. Maybe the thought of war with an alien race was too terrifying to contemplate. The reality, however, was far worse.

It was the year 2130 and I'd been working the lowly role of ship's cook aboard the Starship Pioneer for almost twenty Earth years. The vessel was a research ship primarily, staffed by a team of scientists with a crew of medics, engineers, soldiers, navigators, cooks, and

A is for Aliens

cleaners to support them. Despite being heavily funded by a multi-country initiative, the Pioneer was never expected to return to Earth. The technology was in place to transmit any discoveries back to the command centre, and all aboard fully accepted that this was not a return voyage.

The Pioneer was the fastest and most well-equipped vessel ever created. It was capable of travelling further than humankind had ever gone before and, despite a lengthy list of subjects to study, there was always that one underlying goal - to prove the existence of extra-terrestrial life, even make contact with it. In 2111, when we had first set off, there was an excited buzz aboard The Pioneer. The belief that the scientists would succeed in their mission was strong, but it came with a nervousness. There was no guarantee what obstacles we would face or what danger we could be heading into. The presence of the small team of soldiers should have been a comfort but it had the opposite effect on me. Guns in space were a stupid idea and I saw these men as just trigger-happy grunts, more likely to start a conflict than prevent one. Almost twenty years on and they had let themselves go to the point that they wouldn't be much use against an attack anyway.

The time had taken its toll on the majority of the crew, myself included. Boredom had set in much earlier than I had anticipated. The first few years involved a group of us working our way through the hundreds of books and movies stored in the library, playing each and every board game multiple times, and even sharing beds with one another simply for something to do. Most of us were single, or we wouldn't have agreed to a one-way trip into space, and those few that were married when we left knew there was no point keeping those vows now.

After a few more years it seemed as though everyone had had enough of each other, or at least had run out of things to talk about. People barely spoke, taking care of their jobs in silence, running on autopilot. Fights would break out on occasion as the pressure of being trapped aboard this metal coffin became too much. Two of the crew took their own lives. Excitement and a sense of adventure had been replaced with a feeling of hopelessness, and the low mood was contagious. Even new discoveries that the scientists made, while interesting to begin with, soon lost their appeal. So what if they had discovered a new element within a piece of space rock? Who cares that their equipment picked up traces of water in a planet's atmosphere? Twenty years ago, those discoveries would have been huge. Now, even the researchers didn't seem to care.

This attitude changed in 2030. This discovery got everyone's attention, tearing apart the boredom and filling The Pioneer with something else. Excitement? Nervousness? Fear? You see, I'm not a scientific man. Although I understand the possible implications of discovering water on an alien planet, that in itself doesn't excite me. However, when the research team called an emergency meeting of all personnel, they had something far more interesting to say.

I had switched off the cooker that I'd be slaving over for the past few hours and shuffled along the brightly lit corridors to the meeting room. The room was designed to accommodate all of the crew at one time, but it still felt crowded, perhaps because we had not all been in there together for more than a year. I thought I'd have to feign interest as Reynolds, the lead researcher, began to speak, but the look on his face piqued my curiosity.

Sweat coated the man's forehead and he dabbed at it with a handkerchief. Glancing nervously at the rest of his team, Reynolds cleared his throat. He hadn't aged well, and I briefly thought back to when I first met the man. He must have been on the wrong side of sixty when we left, putting him into his mid-eighties by now. I remember thinking it was optimistic of them to send someone of his age on such a long mission and was thankful that the rest of his team were at least thirty years his junior.

Reynolds tried to speak but the words were drowned out by the murmurs of the crew and I watched as Veronica, his pretty-in-a-nerdy-way assistant pulled a microphone from one of the cupboards and set it up for him. After a piercing screech of feedback, Reynolds managed to get everyone's attention.

"Good afternoon, ladies and gentlemen," he began, his voice quivering with a combination of nerves and age. "As you may have guessed, we have made a

A is for Aliens

discovery of sorts." I glanced around the faces of the crew, most displaying little to no interest, some even conveying annoyance at having been dragged to this meeting.

"I hope it's better than some new type of rock," one of the cleaning crew piped up. There were a few laughs and nods of agreement.

"I don't know if I'd say it's better," Reynolds replied. "But it could certainly be more interesting." The room fell silent as Reynolds continued. "A few hours ago, Mr Stevenson, our chief navigator, spotted something unusual on the radars. Typically, this far into deep space, we only expect to see rocks and comets, and those are few and far between. What Mr Stevenson spotted is something…else." No one spoke, the crowd seeming to hold in a breath at the same time. "Upon closer inspection, we saw that it was a piece of space junk, similar to the pieces of rockets or satellites which become damaged and float off into space."

"So, it's a bit of rubbish? There have been bits of junk floating around the Earth for well over a hundred years. Could it not have floated out here with a

A is for Aliens

hundred years head start?" one of the soldiers asked.

"No," Reynolds replied, and I'm sure he was trying not to roll his eyes. "We are way too far from Earth for it to be man-made. Which, of course, begs the question - where did it come from?"

"What's the plan, then?" the soldier continued. "I assume you want to bring it aboard?"

"I most certainly do," Reynolds replied. "A few of my team, however, have some reservations, so we thought it only fair to explain things in a bit more detail. Veronica, would you mind sharing your concerns?"

Veronica pushed her chair back, causing an uncomfortable scraping sound to echo around the hall. She seemed to mutter a *sorry* before taking the microphone from Reynolds.

"Hi everyone," she began, her nervousness evident. Whether this was related to the discovery or speaking in front of a large crowd I couldn't tell. "So, the item that has come to our attention appears to be around six feet in length, two feet in width, and cylindrical in shape. We have attempted to use our scanning equipment to see inside the item but have had no luck; it appears that the outer material is simply too thick. We have also attempted to scan it for a heat signature but there was not one. These are the standard procedures to determine whether something could be living within this item. Essentially, we've been unable to get a definite answer. There could be nothing in it..."

"Or it could be full of little green men, and we wouldn't know until they were on the ship," the soldier stated.

"In simple terms, you are correct," Reynolds replied to the soldier, taking the microphone from Veronica. "But we have procedures in place for this kind of, erm, event. The capsule would be brought aboard and placed in the isolation chamber. We could then carry out a wide range of tests from inside the laboratory, with no need for anyone to come into contact with it until we were certain it was safe to do so. Of course, our security team would be there to assist, so I'm sure we'll all be perfectly safe." The soldier nodded, looking to the rest of his team for confirmation.

"It's what we're here for," the soldier

stated. "Just let us know what you need."

"Do the rest of us get a say in this?" shouted the cleaner. "I mean, if your own team are scared of that thing then are we at least putting it to a vote?" The question was greeted with nodding heads and murmurs of agreement.

"There will be a vote," Veronica interjected. "But not an individual one, as that would take too long. We want the heads of each department to have their say so could those people stay, and everyone else can return to your stations." This approach didn't seem to go down well with a few people, but on the whole I felt relieved not to have the responsibility of making a decision such as this. I returned to the kitchen and awaited the outcome of the discussion I was not deemed important enough to be a part of.

***

Despite the decision not being unanimous, the majority agreed that the discovery was too important to not investigate further. Reynolds had been vocal in reminding everyone that, should the capsule contain alien life, this had been their main goal when they left Earth and it would mean wasting all these years if they ignored this development simply out of fear. For the first time in a long time, The Pioneer was buzzing with chatter and speculation. The lower ranking crew members, such as myself, relied on gossip which had filtered down the chain to keep us updated as events unfolded.

The capsule was brought through to the isolation chamber, so the main hall and rec rooms were much quieter in the evenings as the cleaners, cooks, and engineers spent their time staring at that metal tube through the viewing windows. Talk from inside the laboratory suggested that the scientists had been unable to identify the material and were still unable to ascertain the contents of the capsule. Word came three days later that they were going to attempt to open it; fortunately for me it was my day off and I couldn't resist going to watch their efforts - it wasn't as though I had anything else to do, anyway. I grabbed a coffee from the self-service machine in the canteen just as Veronica was making herself a tea.

"They're opening that thing up today,

then?" I asked, trying to make conversation.

"Yep," she replied, the worry on her face unmistakable.

"You don't think it's a good idea?" I asked, walking beside her as she headed back to the lab.

"From a scientific point of view, it's absolutely the right thing to do. From a human perspective, it just doesn't feel safe. I mean, it could well be empty, but if it isn't...we have no way of knowing what will be in there and what it could be capable of." I nodded my understanding.

"I'm going to hang out and watch, if that's okay?" I said, knowing that no-one could tell me I couldn't watch from the viewing area. "It's my day off," I added, feeling as though I needed to justify why I was out of the kitchen. Veronica just nodded before she tapped her key-card against the door to the lab and disappeared inside.

The attempts to open the capsule were far less interesting than I had hoped for. I watched Reynolds approach it with three different pieces of equipment, all emitting a high-intensity laser of a different colour, none of which left even a scratch on the shiny surface. Disgruntled and almost crying with frustration, Reynolds called it a night and closed down the lab, plunging the isolation chamber into darkness. I was awoken from my sleep a little after midnight when the sirens began to ring. Every corridor on The Pioneer was illuminated with a red flashing light as I climbed out of bed and opened the door to my small cabin. People ran back and forth in confusion before two soldiers appeared, urging everyone to return to their living quarters and lock the doors. Screams came from the far end of the corridor and I hesitated. My eyes flitted between the perceived safety of my room to the sounds of terror not so far away and I made a choice. Perhaps I could help, or perhaps I would die, but at least it wouldn't be boring.

I walked the corridor slowly, trying my best to assess the upcoming situation. It was difficult to identify any other sounds over the blare of the sirens and the screams of the crew but there was something else...a snapping sound, like bones breaking. I passed the laboratory, and the viewing area for the isolation chamber, and stopped in my tracks. The capsule was no longer sealed; an impossibly dark opening had appeared in the top and I stared at it as the red flashes of the warning lights dragged it from the darkness, a second at a time.

I rounded the corner and slipped, falling to the floor. Everything was red, the lights, the floor, the walls. My feet were coated in the blood of someone, but it was now impossible to tell who they had been. Pieces of flesh were scattered about the corridor alongside torn lab coats and crimson ID badges. The walls were covered in blood spatter and there was even some on the ceiling. Veronica had been right to be afraid of that thing.

Just as I was about to make a run for my cabin, a series of three small flashes accompanied the sound of gunfire nearby, followed by an ear-splitting howl. The soldiers were nearby and, thankfully, seemed to be doing their job. Had they killed whatever had come aboard? I ventured onward, keeping my eyes focused on the next turn in the corridor and away from the mess of body parts which littered the ground. Another gunshot, another howl. The creature was still alive, but it was hurt, at least.

A is for Aliens

I turned the corner as I heard a sickening crunch. One of the soldiers, the last soldier as I quickly discovered, was facing me, his feet dangling a foot off the ground. Holding him in place was what looked like the claw of a scorpion, only much larger, of course. It had pierced his chest from behind and was protruding from the front. I strained in the flashing red lighting to see more details but could not take my eyes from the dying man's face, his mouth gurgling blood, his arms twitching in surrender.

It was not until the creature let the soldier slide from the appendage that I could see what we were facing. I almost let out the most inappropriate of laughs as I surveyed the being that had caused so much destruction, for it looked like an overgrown mantis. It's large, almost perfectly triangular head featured bulbous eyes. Its body was thin but appeared to be entirely made of muscle, supported by strong legs which were as long as the creature was tall. For 'arms' it had the deadly claws which were surprisingly similar to those of a scorpion; sharp, powerful, almost indestructible.

Between the flashes of red light, the

creature could not be seen for the blackness of its exoskeleton was darker than anything I had ever seen. Even when it was illuminated for those brief moments, it was as if it were merely a shadow of a monster, standing among the debris of humankind. If the armed security team could not destroy this beast then the whole ship was doomed, of that I had no doubt, but I still didn't want to go willingly to my death. I ran, or at least I tried to. The floor was slick with the gruesome remains of my fellow travellers and I fell to the floor numerous times. I refused to look at whatever mess my hands landed in each time I hit the floor, choosing to concentrate on keeping ahead of the creature and the awful clicking sound it made.

Soaked in blood which was, thankfully, not my own, I came to a skid at the entrance to the meeting room. I tried the handle, finding it locked, as the clicking sound grew closer. I watched in terror as the two claw-like appendages appeared from around the corner, quickly followed by the rest of that abomination. It was no more than six feet away from me when I felt a hand grab me by the arm and yank me forward.

Veronica had seen me approach the meeting room in which she had been hiding out with another of the science team - a man a little older than me and well within the category of morbidly obese. She had taken a risk by unlocking the door and pulling me to safety, albeit temporary safety, and her colleague was clearly angered by my presence. He explained in hissed whispers how stupid Veronica had been, how it was now every man for himself, and so on. I thought, but had the decency not to say, that if the three of us were to be chased then this chap would make our escape much easier, not to mention keeping that thing fed for some time.

"It seems you were right," I whispered to Veronica.

"I wish I hadn't been," she told me, her eyes tearing up. "Is there anyone else out there?"

"I don't know," I replied. "Lots of people were locking themselves in their cabins, but the soldiers are all dead. They wounded that creature, but it's still fast. It's pretty horrific up by the lab."

"So, what are we supposed to do?"

asked the big guy. "If we can't kill it then we're all going to die! We need to get guns."

"If you feel like going back out there and searching for guns, in the dark, among the leftover pieces of the soldiers, you go ahead," I said, knowing it would be suicide.

"Funny," he replied. "I think I'd rather we go to the ammo room." Veronica and I looked at each other in confusion.

"I thought the soldiers only carried a handgun each, so as not to run the risks that come with having a whole arsenal on a bloody spaceship!" Veronica said.

"You really think they only had a few handguns? I heard them talking before about some high-tech bullets for some new rifles. One of the guys was complaining that they couldn't test them out."

"How come they didn't have them tonight?" I asked. "If they had better weapons, why not actually use them when they were needed?"

"He's talking shit," Veronica said. "Our best chance is to stay here and keep out of sight."

"Until when?" her colleague demanded.

"Until we starve? Until we're the last ones left, and we just wait for a fucking alien to break in and kill us? We have to try something." And, for the first time, I had to agree with the guy.

"He's right," I said, looking at Veronica as best I could in the darkness. "But I'll go. You're safer in here for now, and you..." I paused as I turned to face the huge man, "...you'll slow me down. Just tell me where this ammo store is." He didn't even try to go with me, and I wondered if sending me had been his plan all along.

"When I say ammo room, it's more of a cupboard than a room, I think. I've never actually seen it. I just heard the guys talking about it a while ago. But I'm sure it's near the soldiers' quarters, and it won't say what it is on the door."

"Helpful," I replied, approaching the exit to the meeting room. I pressed my ear against the door, listening for any more of that awful clicking but heard nothing. In my head I planned my route, knowing that my best chance for survival was to get there quickly and locked into the ammo room. If the creature followed then so be it, at least I'd be armed. *Open the door, run to the left, past my cabin and on to the lift, down one level, follow the corridor to the right.* I'd only been past the soldier's quarters once before and had laughed at how overly macho it had been. The rest of The Pioneer was immaculate but those few cabins had been decorated like a teenage boy's bedroom, with posters of topless women holding ridiculously large guns, sports cars, and military vehicles. I racked my brain to locate any other rooms along there but came up short. *Only one way to find out.*

I gave Veronica a curt nod as I gently opened the door, holding my breath as it let out a small creak. No sound aside from the blare of the alarm could be heard so I stepped into the corridor. I glanced around, took a deep breath, and ran as fast as I could. The carnage was far less in this direction, leading me to believe that the monster had headed back to where I had met it, presumably to feast on what flesh remained.

I reached the lift safely, hitting the call button and staring into the darkness from whence I had come, expecting to see claws emerge from the shadows. Nothing came for me, not even the lift, which I presumed was a safety protocol triggered by the alarms sounding. The stairwell was only a few feet further, so I reached it in a matter of seconds and began to descend the metal steps, my shoes clanging against them noisily. One floor meant eighteen steps in two sections of nine and, when I reached the level I needed, a thought hit me. The shape of the creature's legs and its overall size made me question its ability to follow me down here. Perhaps that thing could be contained to one floor, at least for now.

I hurried along, checking each door that I passed. Each of the soldiers' cabins were unlocked and uninhabited. At the far end, as the corridor turned to the right, there were two more doors. One was labelled as a cleaner's stockroom, presumably for mops, cleaning products, cloths, and the like. The other just carried a warning of high voltage and a clear *Keep Out* sign. With no doubt in my mind, I pulled at the door, but it refused to budge. *Of course it'd be locked up securely,* I thought, hardly daring to consider where the key would be kept. *If it's not in the security chief's room, then it must have been on his person and that's as good as lost.*

I quickly made my way through the

cabins, trying to discover which belonged to the Chief of Security. I never found out which room was his, just as I never discovered the whereabouts of the key, and I never found out if that door really did lead to an ammo supply. So many unanswered questions. The one question that I now *did* have an answer to related to the creature's ability to manoeuvre itself down stairs. It stood at the foot of the stairwell, its impossible blackness a silhouette of terror in the dark, building up to a crescendo of clicking. I could try to run, but what was the point? We weren't getting into the weapons stash, we couldn't isolate this thing on one floor and just carry on our existence as though it wasn't there. For all I knew, I was the last human left on The Pioneer. Fear turned to relief as I faced that thing head on. I knew it was futile, but I no longer cared. That monster, that alien, brought with it an end to the boredom. Even so, I managed a smile at the knowledge we had succeeded in our mission, even if that success was not quite as everyone had hoped. We had discovered the existence of extra-terrestrial life and I'm sure that Reynolds, especially at his age, died a happy man

A is for Aliens

with this knowledge.

I charged at the creature, intending to land blows on its bony exoskeleton but I never made it that far. It stuck out one clawed limb just as I got close enough and I felt it glide through my chest and tear free from my back. I felt, more than heard, the crack of my ribs as they shattered, and felt myself choking on the warm, metallic blood which now flowed freely. I looked into the creature's eyes as it tilted its head, appearing to examine me, and then nothing but darkness.

A is for Aliens

Even in Darkness, We See Them

Megan Neumann

Maddy lingered by Brady's bedside, tucking in his covers a little too tightly. She didn't want to leave his side, didn't want to go to her own bed. As she leaned in to kiss his forehead, he reached out his hand and tugged on her sleeve. "There are men in my room at night," he said, his voice low, his eyes steady and serious.

"Men?" Maddy asked. Alarm, followed quickly by amusement, went through her mind in seconds. Kids dreamed. The lines between reality and imagination blurred, especially in the darkness of night. She knew this better than most people. "You've never said anything about men in your room before."

"I forgot until now," Brady whispered. He furrowed his brow, and to Maddy he resembled a tiny old man, too wise and too thoughtful to be her six-year-old son. "But I remembered just now when you were standing over me. They come in there." He pointed over Maddy's shoulder. "Through the wall. Then they poke me. They pull my hair." Brady's eyes looked through her as if he could see the dream men over her shoulder. "I can't move when they're here. I don't like it." His voice started to rise. Maddy sensed his temper rising too. She placed her hands on his shoulder.

"Shh," Maddy said. "There are no men. It was just a dream."

He sighed. Maddy's mother sighed the same way whenever Maddy said something particularly dense. Maddy rolled her eyes, the same way she did when her mother sighed at her.

"It's not a dream, Mom!" he yelled, and Maddy knew nothing she could do would stop his fit. He would grab the sheets in his fists and kick the blanket, crying out for Maddy to leave, pleading for her to leave him alone forever, screaming about how she was hurting him.

Somehow, remarkably, he took a breath and looked up at Maddy with old man eyes, eyes with too much knowledge. How could she have a son so smart when her own life was riddled with dumb mistake after dumb mistake?

"I know it's not a dream," he said. "I saw them. Their bodies are made of static except for their teeth. Their teeth are like ours. They're always smiling."

A is for Aliens

"Static? With teeth? That can't be real, can it?" Maddy tried to make her voice light, joking, so he'd know there was nothing to fear. "Sometimes dreams can seem real." Maddy turned on the lamp on his bedside table. "They can look just like real life, but they're not real. No one comes in here at night but me and your grandma." She kissed his clammy forehead. "I can leave the lamp on if you get scared."

"It doesn't matter." His voice was resigned. "Light or dark, it doesn't matter."

"How do you know?" Maddy asked, feigning curiosity. "Light makes scary things disappear." She smiled, while lying through her teeth.

"Last time the lamp was on, and they were still here. It didn't make them go away. They pulled out my hair."

At these words, Maddy's eyes widened. "Look at me."

His gray eyes moved upward, gazing into Maddy's own brown eyes. He wore a solemn expression.

"There are no men. I know you think it's real, but it's not." She brushed Brady's hair from his forehead. "You have to accept that." She moved toward him and breathed in the smell of his shampoo. His downy hair brushed against her cheek.

A is for Aliens

She wanted to hold him, but she knew he wouldn't let her. In the last year, he started to hate hugs from his mom. He was too big now, he liked to say. Big kids didn't hug their moms.

"Sometimes I have bad dreams too, and you know how I deal with it?"

"How?" For an instant, his voice was petulant, more like a six-year-old's voice should be.

"I close my eyes and go back to sleep." Maddy didn't blink as she lied. "Can you do that?"

He nodded, and Maddy tightened the blanket around his body one last time before leaving him.

In their living room, her mother, Carol, lay across the sofa watching reruns of sitcoms. Carol liked the familiarity of the programs she'd seen dozens of times. Maddy couldn't blame her. She too found comfort in knowing when to laugh and when to cry.

"That took longer than usual," Carol said. "Didn't have a fit again, did he?"

"No, thank God. But he's having nightmares. Apparently, static men come into his bedroom at night. Static men with teeth."

"Static men? That's a new one. You used to have nightmares, remember?"

A is for Aliens

"I do."

"His will pass. Just like yours did."

Maddy said nothing. Her mother couldn't see the pain on Maddy's face because Carol still faced the television, the bright pictures lighting her features.

Should Maddy have told her mother the truth? No, she knew she shouldn't. What good would the truth do in this family?

The nightmares never did go away. Instead, she learned to live with them. In the night, when she sweated through her sheets, her heart pounding, knowing someone was in the room with her, she would close her eyes and hope sleep would come again soon. But Maddy couldn't tell her mother that. Carol would feel guilty, just as Maddy felt guilty over not saving Brady from his own nightmares.

"I'm going to bed," Maddy said. Carol grunted in reply.

In the kitchen, Maddy took her sleeping pills and instantly a wave of relief rushed over her. It was impossible for the pills to take effect so quickly, but she felt an easy lightness upon taking the drug anyway. Maddy drifted in a daze to her bed, passing by Brady's room, the light of his lamp shining beneath the door. She paused, pressed her body against the

A is for Aliens

doorframe, and listened. No sounds. He'd always been a quiet sleeper.

Over the next few days Brady didn't mention his nightmares again. His days passed as usual, a lonesome boy playing in his room. But there was something different about him. He seemed quieter. Was he growing paler and thinner? Some days he went to the backyard and played on a rusted swing set with only one swing and a slide that tipped to one side when he sat on it. Maddy knew she should get rid of it, but he loved the set so much. Besides, she couldn't afford a new one.

As usual, when she'd leave for work, Carol would watch him. That weekend Maddy heard all about the tantrums during the week, his fits of selfishness or hatefulness toward his grandmother.

"He'll grow out of it," Maddy said. "He's just a difficult boy."

"He's a problem. What are you going to do next year when he has to go to school?"

Maddy shrugged. "I'm sure there are other kids like him."

Carol sighed. "They'll kick him out of school. They'll call you during the day to come get him if he kicks and bites and screams like he's been doing. What will

A is for Aliens

you do if they start asking questions about him?"

"What do you want me to do?" Maddy asked. Her mother knew she spent all her free time with Brady. She tried to make him good. Sometimes she worried he was unreachable, a distant star too far away or too hot for her to touch. No matter how hard she tried to grasp him, he eluded her. This distant boy would never be hers.

"You need to discipline him." Carol crossed her arms and set her jaw.

"Like you disciplined me?" Maddy said this with more vitriol than she'd intended.

"Yeah, I brought the belt out more than a few times in your day, and you turned out all right."

"Did I?"

Carol stared at her daughter, her eyes searching Maddy's eyes. Maddy wondered how her mother could ever think she'd turned out all right.

"Single mother. Shit job. Shit house. Still living with my mom. Yeah, I turned out great. And it's all because of your fine parenting. It's your fault I even have Brady."

Carol slapped her. Maddy's face flew to the side, her cheek burning hot. She clutched her face and let out a small sob. She didn't want Carol to see her crying, so

A is for Aliens

she turned and watched Brady through the kitchen window. He'd climbed up the side of the swing set and had somehow made it to the top horizontal bar, straddling it with his feet dangling over each side. It wasn't safe. He would fall and break an arm or worse. But Maddy didn't want to be one of those parents who never let their kids get dirty or scrape their knees. She wanted him to learn on his own. Maybe she'd given him too much space. Maybe he'd learned too much. But he looked so happy.

"I did as much as I could with you," Carol said quietly. "You're doing as much as you can with him. We're all doing our best with the lives we've chosen."

"I didn't choose this."

As Maddy tucked Brady into bed again, she asked him if he still had nightmares.

"I don't have nightmares," Brady said matter-of-factly.

"You had a nightmare a few nights ago about men coming into your room. Remember?"

He pursed his lips. "Mom. I told you it wasn't a nightmare." He was so disappointed in Maddy's stupidity. "But *you* didn't believe me. You *never* believe

A is for Aliens

me. Like when I told you about the lady from before—"

"Hush." Maddy pressed a finger over his lips. "I told you she wasn't real either. You're still having nightmares, aren't you? You're still seeing the static men."

He nodded. "I saw them last night. I'm used to them now. They don't scare me."

This surprised Maddy. How could he not be afraid?

"You're not scared of the men who look like static?"

"They're not really static. I looked at them closer. Their skin won't hold still. It floats. But their teeth are normal. And they have no lips, so that's why they're always smiling."

Maddy imagines this, and a chill rushes through her.

"Do they ever talk to you?"

"No. They like to watch me and touch my skin. I think they're scientists."

Maddy wondered how he even knew what scientists were. Or what static was. Then again, she remembered, he watched so much TV. He memorized everything. He probably knew more than she did.

"Why would they study you?"

"I asked them that, but they didn't answer."

A is for Aliens

Maddy couldn't get the image of the static men out of her mind, so it didn't surprise her when she dreamed about them that night. It didn't feel like a dream, though. At first, she didn't see them. A light emanated from the corner of the room. Then the light grew, moving closer. She couldn't move her body. Their breathing sounded like rushing wind through leaves, growing louder till the sound was like a train. She wished she could scream, but her throat was closed.

They stood over her. Their skin moved over their organs like wisps of smoke, ever changing without feature except for their wide smiling mouths. Her heart thumped in her chest. Her fingers twitched. Her fingers were the only part of her she could move. But fingers were useless without moving hands and arms.

The static men moved their own hands in motions through the air and lights appeared before them. The lights blinked like camera flashes.

She must get up.

What if they were in Brady's room too? What if they take him away from her?

She tried to move her arms again, but her limbs were heavy, too heavy to move. She struggled until she had lifted one arm, but the weight pulled it to the bed again.

A is for Aliens

She opened her mouth and started to scream, but the sound came out in a low croaking. Maddy wondered if this sound had actually come from her.

Screams erupted from somewhere in the house. Was it Brady's room? Maddy couldn't turn her head to listen. She couldn't move her legs to run to him.

Above her, the static men laid their translucent hands over her body and moved them up and down. She felt no pain. Not even an unpleasantness. Their touches were soft, gentle. It wasn't until they pulled the hairs from Maddy's head that she felt any discomfort at all.

Then they were gone, and the screaming stopped.

"You look like hell." Carol set a cup of coffee in front of Maddy.

"Thanks, Mom." She sipped the coffee, not really tasting it or smelling it. She hadn't tasted or smelt anything in days, not since the static men started visiting her.

Beside her at the kitchen table, Brady sat eating his cereal in silence. His skin was sallow. Maddy touched her palm to his forehead. He felt too cold.

"Are you feeling okay?" she asked him.

A is for Aliens

He spooned more cereal into his mouth and chewed silently.

"You haven't been sleeping?" she asked him.

He shook his head. "They keep waking me up," he mumbled, looking down at the bowl, stirring the milk until he'd created a little whirlpool. Maddy watched it spin.

"He still having nightmares?" Carol asked.

"I should take him to a doctor." Maddy looked up at her mother, but Carol looked skeptical.

"You really want to get involved with something like that? Doctors ask a lot of questions. What if they ask too many questions and someone finds out too much?"

"I've got to do something. I'm not sleeping either now."

"You taking your medicine?" Carol asked.

"Yeah, but it doesn't matter."

"It doesn't matter," Brady repeated. "They'll come no matter what."

"What the fuck are you talking about, boy?"

"Mom!" Maddy yelled. "Language!"

Carol cackled. "He's heard worse."

Maddy moved toward Brady and whispered, "I believe you. They're real. I've seen them in my room. I'm not going to let them hurt you again."

"They don't hurt me, Mom. I told you. They're just curious."

"I heard you screaming," Maddy said.

"That wasn't me. It was you."

When Maddy was younger, she assumed everyone else was the same as her—everyone was scared to go to sleep. Sleep was dangerous and should be avoided at all cost. She assumed this was normal, so she didn't tell Carol about it for years. She grew so sick. Maddy knew Carol used to worry over her as if expecting her to die at any moment.

Now, as an adult, it was Maddy's turn to worry. Just like Carol, she worried her own son would leave her too.

But the static men were not the same as her old nightmares. Her old nightmares were quick flashes of things she'd left behind, things she had once loved taken from her. Bad things that had happened.

How could she stop the creatures paralyzing her? Night after night, she struggled under their control while they caressed, prodded, poked, and violated her sleep. Her days dragged by in painful episodes of half wakefulness. She had to go to work, had to continue her life and provide for her son. At the same time, she was failing him and failing herself. She'd die from lack of sleep, she knew. Then Brady would be left to Carol and to them, these static men who wanted to torture her and her son on a nightly basis.

"The static men are worried about you," Brady said one night as they sat together at the table, neither of them eating.

"How do you know?"

"They told me."

"But they don't speak. Or they didn't. Have they spoken to you?"

"Not really. Not like how we're talking now. But sometimes they want me to know what they're thinking, and I do."

Somehow this made sense to Maddy. Of course, the static men could communicate without words.

"Why should they be worried about me? If they are, maybe they should leave us alone. I was fine before they came into our lives."

"The static men say that it's not them you're afraid of. You're afraid of the past. They say it haunts you and you won't face it."

"The static men don't know what they're talking about."

"The static men know everything," Brady said.

"They can't know everything."

Brady stared at her, his face unmoving. Then he folded his hands in his lap and looked out the open window where his rusty swing swayed slightly in the wind, its chains creaking.

"The static men have helped me remember," Brady said. "That lady before. I remember her now."

Maddy's blood became cold. She took a quick breath and stood quickly, knocking over her chair. She backed away and nearly tripped. "I have to go. Your grandmother is calling."

"She's not my grandmother."

Maddy didn't acknowledge this. Instead, she stumbled through the dark house, the hall and rooms suddenly too small, the ceiling too low. Had the house always felt so claustrophobic? Soon she was in her mother's bedroom. Her mother who was not her mother at all. Just like she was not Brady's mother.

Carol's body was sprawled out across the bed, the limbs awkwardly posed around her head. Briefly, Maddy thought the old woman was dead, but then she saw her mother's heavy chest rise and fall, her eyelids flicker. Most likely dream

A is for Aliens

images filled the old woman's head, probably far more pleasant than anything Maddy had dreamt in the last two weeks.

"He knows," Maddy announced.

Carol didn't stir.

Maddy moved quickly, pouncing on the bed, grabbing her mother's shoulders between her hands, shaking the old woman until her bloodshot eyes opened and gazed confusedly up at Maddy.

"What is it?"

"He knows!" The words came out hissed, but loud, loud enough for Brady to hear if he decided to stand in the hall listening.

"Who knows what?"

"Brady! He knows the truth. He knows what we did to him!"

"So?" Carol sat up. She pushed Maddy away and breathed slowly. Maddy saw no anxiety in Carol's face, whereas Maddy's heart pounded quickly in her chest. She wondered if her mother could hear it. Then she cursed herself for thinking that word: mother. Carol was not her mother. No more than she was Brady's mother and now he knew. And Carol didn't seem to care.

"He's just a boy," Carol said. "He can't do anything. We have the paperwork now. He's ours."

"But what if he tells someone!"

A is for Aliens

"Who will he tell? And so what if he does? No one will believe him. Kids make up stories. We'll tell them he was dreaming it like the static men he dreamt up."

Maddy felt her dread receding. She put her face into her palms and took several deep breaths. The first few came out ragged, but slowly, her breathing steadied. Her mother was right. Her mother had always been right. Carol had never gotten caught when she took Maddy. There had never even been any close calls, as far as Maddy knew. And they had never gotten caught with Brady.

Three years ago they took him from his front yard. His real mother had been on the phone inside the house, probably gossiping with another one of the mothers whose house was perfect and new with a yard perfectly manicured by a paid stranger. God forbid the woman actually dirty her own hands. God forbid the woman actually watch her son.

Well, Maddy would watch him. She'd love him, and he would be hers, just like she had been Carol's.

Carol had encouraged her to take him, told her this was their family way. What kind of person would the boy grow up to

A is for Aliens

be in the clutches of some vain woman who never showed affection, not genuine affection at least?

And Maddy had been so lonely. It'd be so nice to have something of her own to hold and love her.

They took the boy on a hot summer's evening while crickets chirped and sprinklers rained down on the green lawns. Brady didn't even cry when Maddy picked him up. He smiled at her, a wise, knowing smile that would become so familiar, yet still strange over the years to come.

Then they drove through the night, across four states, never once stopping. No one saw them; no one knew where the boy had gone. She thought they had gotten away with it.

"You're right," Maddy said quietly. "How can he even know for sure?"

"Go talk to him," Carol said, holding Maddy's hand, squeezing her fingers too tightly. "Tell him he's had another dream. Tell him the nightmares aren't real. You are his mother!" These last few words she spat out, perhaps convincing herself more than Maddy.

"I am his mother," Maddy said.

A is for Aliens

Then she walked into the hall and saw the light on in Brady's room. She was prepared to tell him what her mother had told her to say. But instead, when she saw the boy curled up in his blankets, a book propped up on his knees, she couldn't bring herself to lie. Who was she kidding? He was no son of hers. She loved him, yes. Perhaps he loved her as well. But they were not blood. They were not the same. The only things they'd ever share were the facts that they had both been taken and they had both seen the static men.

"I am not your real mother," she said.

"I know," Brady said. "I've known for a long time. Even before the static men, I knew."

"How?"

"I could tell." He looked up from his book and stared solemnly. "We're not the same."

"I love you. You know that, don't you?"

"I know you love me," he said, "but what you did was wrong. You broke the law."

"Breaking the law is wrong. I don't deny it." Maddy sat on the bed and took his hands into her own. "Listen, I know I did something wrong, but it's too late to make it right. I'm sorry for what I did. I'm sorry every day. What I did, it haunts me. I have nightmares about it. I can't sleep."

A is for Aliens

"The static men say you're troubled. But for other reasons."

"What have the static men told you about me?"

"They know Grandma isn't your real mom. You were taken too late, and because of that, you're troubled. Troubled like her. It's a long line of trouble, they say, but they think I'll be okay since I was younger. I'm adjusted. And you could still make it right."

"What do you mean?"

"They've been studying us. The static men want to know about us. About people. They're here to understand what we'd be like if they took people like you took me. And like Grandma took you. They said they were studying how we'd do if we were taken. They don't think you'll make it, but I will. I'm stronger."

Maddy's hands began to shake. "What do they mean I won't make it?"

Brady shook his head. "You know what they mean, Mom."

Maddy didn't want to think about *not making it.* She'd avoided thinking about it her whole life. She stood, backed out of the room, and walked down the hall to her own room where she collapsed onto her bed face first. The anger and confusion she felt quickly subsided, overcome by deep exhaustion. She felt herself dozing. She shook her head quickly. No, she couldn't fall asleep. The static men would come if she did.

The static men. They thought they knew her. They thought they knew what would become of her life, but they didn't. They couldn't. They weren't real. It was a shared hallucination between her and Brady.

She thought of their long, unsubstantial fingers, reaching out to her, wiggling before her paralyzed body. The horror of it. In those moments, she'd only think of the worst memories from her youth, the paralyzing fear she'd felt when Carol had taken her. She was six, had just started kindergarten. It was after school when she'd been taken, picked up by Carol, lured into the car by some weak lie.

As the static men probed her, she saw Carol's big fist coming down hard, hitting her right in the jaw, knocking her to the floor of the car where she'd lay for another ten hours, peeing herself, weeping quietly, hoping the strange woman wouldn't hit her again. Carol kept threatening to throw her out of the car while it was moving, telling her the trucks would run over her and smear her across the road. So she better not make a sound. She better not

A is for Aliens

act up or talk to anyone when they stopped for gas.

Every night for years, she'd wake up sweating, feeling as though she were still lying on that floorboard, her body jolted with each bump in the road, snot drying on her upper lip. She couldn't stand being in the darkness of her room, so she'd always leave a light on in her bathroom or small lamp beside her bed. In the darkness, she felt she was still a child being taken, curled up and afraid to move. In the darkness, she could see the horrors of her past clearly.

Now Carol slept in the room next to her, and Maddy realized she'd fallen asleep. The static men stood over her. But something was different this time. Her body felt loose, not like the stiff paralysis normally experienced during their visits. She wiggled her toes to test it. Then she lifted a foot.

She stood cautiously, watching the static men. They were watching her too. There were six of them, and they stood about five feet away, not dancing like normal, not wiggling their fingers before her face. One lifted a hand and beckoned her forward. They turned in unison and walked down the hall. She followed.

A is for Aliens

She expected them to go to Brady's room, but instead, they turned left into Carol's bedroom. She joined them there where they made a semicircle around Carol's bed. Each of the static men pointed at Carol. Then they looked at Maddy, if they could look. They had no eyes, just blank, static faces interrupted by wide toothy smiles.

"What?" Maddy asked. "What do you want me to do?"

"It's too late for you," Brady said behind her. She turned and saw him standing in the doorway.

"They say it's not too late for me. I'll be all right. But you, you're haunted."

"I'm haunted by these things!" she yelled, thrusting a hand toward the static men. "They're ruining my life! Our lives! We were fine before all this started to happen."

"No, Mom. You've never been fine. You've got to do what's right. The static men are trying to tell you. You'll never be okay. You were too old when you were taken. You're messed up, Mom. But you can still save me. You have to do it."

"Do what?" She spat this question, and as she did, Carol stirred on the bed.

Maddy watched Carol open her eyes slowly, look around blearily, and then sit

A is for Aliens

up, her eyes opening wide and darting around the room.

"What is this?" Carol asked.

Around her, the static men hissed, though their smiles never faltered.

"What are you doing in my room? Can't you let an old woman sleep? Get back to your room and take that boy with you!"

The hissing grew louder. Maddy felt as if she were standing in the middle of a beehive.

Brady stepped forward and tugged on Maddy's sleeve. "The static men say she won't let me go. They say she won't let you go either. You've got to stop it. You'll sleep better when you do."

"What is this idiot talking about? Get him out of here, and you get out too!" Carol roared, but Brady and Maddy stood still. The static men were moving in. They started their dance, wiggling their fingers before Carol's face.

"What are they doing?" Maddy asked. "Move, Mom!"

Carol stepped out of bed and walked through the static men. They followed her, circling closely.

"She can't see them, can she?" Maddy whispered. "Are they really there?'

"They don't want her to see them," Brady said, quietly.

A is for Aliens

"Listen," Carol said, moving close and poking a finger hard against Maddy's chest, "I'm sick of this nonsense. Both of you won't speak of this again. You'll act normal as if nothing's wrong. Because nothing is wrong, is it?"

Maddy shook her head slowly. "Everything is wrong. Nothing has ever been right in this house."

Carol slapped Maddy. Maddy instinctively rubbed her cheek and bowed her head. It wasn't the first time Carol had slapped her. But perhaps it would be the last.

"The static men say you can be all right?" Maddy whispered to Brady. "Because you're young enough."

"Yes," Brady said. "I'll be all right. I'll go home. Do it, Mom. They'll help you."

"What is this weird little shit saying?" Carol spat. She grabbed Brady by his wrist and yanked him toward her. "What the fuck are you yammering on about, you little freak!" She grabbed a fistful of his hair, and he cried out.

"Stop it!" Maddy reached forward. Carol slapped her again but this time harder. Maddy stumbled backward, falling to the floor. She felt the sudden panic of being trapped as a child. She wanted to curl up, pull her knees close to her chest, and pray

A is for Aliens

for it to all be over soon. Then she heard Brady yell. He was still strong. Maddy wouldn't let Carol weaken him, break him as she had broken Maddy so long ago.

"I'll do it," Maddy said quietly. "But you have to help me." She nodded toward the static men.

The static men obliged. She saw them wiggle their long fingers around Carol's body. Carol let out a strangled, "Gnnuhhh," sound. Then she collapsed onto the floor, her body stiffened.

Maddy leaped on top of the woman she'd called mother for so long, but she'd always known, always hated. This woman was no mother. This woman had taken her from her home, put fear into her heart, and forced Maddy to do the same thing twenty years later. Now Maddy's life was haunted, tainted by the stain of her own crimes.

Maddy wrapped her fingers—short and stubby compared to the static men's—around Carol's neck.

Carol did not fight back. She was paralyzed just as Maddy had been all those nights.

Maddy hoped her mother could see the static men, smiling down as they wiggled their fingers. She hoped, too, Carol remembered the horrors she'd committed,

A is for Aliens

saw them flashing before her eyes as they did so often when Maddy closed her own.

Maddy drove through the night. She hadn't forgotten his real name. She'd kept newspaper clippings from right after she'd taken him, kept track of the search for him. She knew where his family had moved when his real parents divorced. She supposed they couldn't handle the sadness of it, losing their child.

Maddy suspected she wouldn't be able to handle it either. But it didn't matter. Carol's body would be found soon, and Maddy would confess. She'd pay for her crimes like she deserved. That was fine with her. After she'd leave him at the doorstep of his mother's house, she'd drive through the night and return to her bedroom, waiting for the police to come for her. There, she'd close her eyes in her own bedroom, and for once in her life, in the darkness, she'd see nothing at all.

Also from Red Cape Publishing

Anthologies:

Elements of Horror Book One: Earth
Elements of Horror Book Two: Air
Elements of Horror Book Three: Fire
Elements of Horror Book Four: Water
A is for Aliens: A-Z of Horror Book One
B is for Beasts: A-Z of Horror Book Two
C is for Cannibals: A-Z of Horror Book Three
D is for Demons: A-Z of Horror Book Four
E is for Exorcism: A-Z of Horror Book Five
F is for Fear: A-Z of Horror Book Six
G is for Genies: A-Z of Horror Book Seven
H is for Hell: A-Z of Horror Book Eight
I is for Internet: A-Z of Horror Book Nine
J is for Jack-o'-Lantern: A-Z of Horror Book Ten
K is for Kidnap: A-Z of Horror Book Eleven
L is for Lycans: A-Z of Horror Book Twelve
M is for Medical: A-Z of Horror Book Thirteen
N is for Nautical: A-Z of Horror Book Fourteen
It Came from the Darkness: A Charity Anthology
Out of the Shadows: A Charity Anthology
Castle Heights: 18 Storeys, 18 Stories
Sweet Little Chittering
Unceremonious
The Nookienomicon

Short Story Collections:

Embrace the Darkness by P.J. Blakey-Novis
Tunnels by P.J. Blakey-Novis
The Artist by P.J. Blakey-Novis
Karma by P.J. Blakey-Novis
The Place Between Worlds by P.J. Blakey-Novis
Home by P.J. Blakey-Novis
Short Horror Stories by P.J. Blakey-Novis
Short Horror Stories Vol.2 by P.J. Blakey-Novis
Keep It Inside & Other Weird Tales by Mark Anthony Smith
Everything's Annoying by J.C. Michael
Six! By Mark Cassell
Monsters in the Dark by Donovan 'Monster' Smith
Barriers by David F. Gray
Love & Other Dead Things by Astrid Addams
Bone Carver by Gemma Paul

Novelettes:

The Ivory Tower by Antoinette Corvo

Novellas:

Four by P.J. Blakey-Novis
Dirges in the Dark by Antoinette Corvo
The Cat That Caught the Canary by Antoinette Corvo
Bow-Legged Buccaneers from Outer Space by David Owain Hughes
Spiffing by Tim Mendees
A Splintered Soul by Adrian Meredith
Scavengers of the Sun by Adrian Meredith

Novels:

Madman Across the Water by Caroline Angel
The Curse Awakens by Caroline Angel
Less by Caroline Angel
Where Shadows Move by Caroline Angel
Origin of Evil by Caroline Angel
Origin of Evil: Beginnings by Caroline Angel
The Vegas Rift by David F. Gray
The Broken Doll by P.J. Blakey-Novis
The Broken Doll: Shattered Pieces by P.J. Blakey-Novis
South by Southwest Wales by David Owain Hughes
Any Which Way but South Wales by David Owain Hughes
Appletown by Antoinette Corvo
Nails by K.J. Sargeant

Art Books:

Demons Never Die by David Paul Harris & P.J. Blakey-Novis
Six Days of Violence by P.J Blakey-Novis & David Paul Harris

Follow Red Cape Publishing

www.redcapepublishing.com
www.facebook.com/redcapepublishing
www.twitter.com/redcapepublish
www.instagram.com/redcapepublishing
www.pinterest.co.uk/redcapepublishing
www.patreon.com/redcapepublishing
www.ko-fi.com/redcape
www.buymeacoffee.com/redcape

Printed in Great Britain
by Amazon